─────────────── ★ ───────────────

"GOOD THING WE AIN'T NERVOUS TYPES."

"Nervous?" Mitch Bushyhead questioned.

"The type to see the supernatural in everything that happens."

"Ghosts, you mean."

"Not that I believe in that nonsense, o'course."

"Of course."

"Still," Duck mused, "it's mighty odd, Graham Thornton dying outside the lodge and so close to those woods, with all the rumors that have been going around—about the lodge being on an Indian graveyard and Cherokee witches being upset about it."

"Duck, it wasn't a witch who tinkered with Thornton's insulin."

"I know that," Duck said a bit huffily. "I'm just saying it's strange."

Mitch nodded, reflecting that Duck wouldn't be the only one to remark upon the coincidence.

─────────────── ★ ───────────────

"This is Hillerman with an Oklahoma accent."

—*The Purloined Letter*

"A very intricate whodunit."

—*Mystery News*

Also available from Worldwide Mystery by
JEAN HAGER

THE GRANDFATHER MEDICINE

NIGHT WALKER

JEAN HAGER

W❖RLDWIDE ®

TORONTO • NEW YORK • LONDON • PARIS
AMSTERDAM • STOCKHOLM • HAMBURG
ATHENS • MILAN • TOKYO • SYDNEY

For Kenneth,
whose love and strength
have sustained me for so many years.

NIGHT WALKER

A Worldwide Mystery/December 1991

First published by St. Martin's Press Incorporated.

ISBN 0-373-26085-7

Acknowledgments

For assisting me in understanding the dangers and treatment of diabetes, I wish to thank John Sacra, M.D., Medical Director, Trauma/Emergency Center, and Dwight Vance, R.Ph., Drug Information Specialist, Saint Francis Hospital, Tulsa, Oklahoma.

ONE

Monday, December 11
5:30 p.m.

JOY YEAKY had been on duty for two hours when the snow started. An hour and half later it showed no signs of letting up. Beyond the glass-fronted foyer the snow had wiped out familiar landmarks. The parking lot, surrounded by beds of holly and blue spruce, the long lawn sloping down to the shore of the lake, now seemed strange. She felt isolated in an empty and frozen place.

There wouldn't be many check-ins in this weather, she thought, and it would be more than four hours before she could go home. She was manning the desk alone, so there wasn't even anyone to talk to. She sighed and returned to reading her novel.

Graham Thornton walked up to the desk. She recognized his measured tread on the flagstone floor, but she kept her head bowed over her book, pretending she hadn't heard. Ignore him and maybe he'll go away.

He leaned over her and blew on the back of her neck. His warm breath turned into a cold trickle shivering down her spine.

"Perfect afternoon to spend in bed."

She should have known ignoring him wouldn't work. She looked up and blinked as though startled. He had a long, lantern-jawed face, pale gray eyes under heavy lids, a hoarse voice considered by women to be sexy. Her stomach tightened, but she kept her voice cool and impersonal. "The radio weatherman said we're in for much more snow. It could break the twelve-inch record."

The gray eyes held silvery amusement—or was it contempt?—as he said abruptly, "Come to my suite in twenty minutes." He turned away without waiting for a response.

"I can't leave the desk."

"Ask Billy Choate to spell you. The waiters are standing around twiddling their thumbs this afternoon."

"I'd rather not."

His head snapped back around. "Excuse me?"

"What'll I tell him?"

"Whatever you want to tell him. Just do it."

She clamped her lips together in a furious line as he walked away, swaggering a little. Arrogant jerk. All right, she'd deliver the news when they were alone in his suite. First thing. If he fired her, he'd just have to fire her. But there was a sick flutter in her stomach at the thought.

Maybe it wouldn't come to that. In any case, she'd reached the point where anxiety over losing her job had been outweighed by a growing awareness of her folly and what could come of it. The queasy stirring of her stomach increased.

SHE SAT ON THE EDGE of the bed, buttoning her blouse. She felt used and tossed aside like a disposable diaper. He'd grabbed her roughly the instant she'd stepped into the suite, hadn't given her a chance to say anything before he was all over her. Imagine, she'd once been flattered by his eager attacks—there was no other word for them—couplings devoid of any tenderness. He actually thought he was a great lover! No wonder his wife was divorcing him.

The first few times the recklessness of it had seemed exciting. But she hadn't felt anything for weeks now except disgust and fear that Larry would find out. How could she have been so stupid?

Only the worry that she'd lose her job had kept her silent this long. With Larry in welding school full-time, they couldn't get along without her paycheck. But there were other jobs. If worse came to worse, they could move in with her parents for a while.

She despised her cowardice in letting it happen again. What was wrong with her? "I can't do this anymore."

The draperies were drawn, and the bedroom was dim and depressing. He was sitting in a black leather slingback chair, tying his shoes, and he scowled darkly without looking up. "What do you mean, you can't?"

"It's too risky."

"Life is full of risks."

"I don't want to jeopardize my marriage."

He jerked at his shoestring and stood. He stabbed a finger at the air. "It's not over till I say it's over. You try to walk out on me, I'll make sure your old man knows all about us. Understand?"

Feeling the blood leave her face, she stared at him. Her nausea intensified, turning her stomach into a roiling ball of fear. Hard, slitted eyes held her gaze for a moment before he walked out.

The gold wristwatch Larry had given her last Christmas lay on the bedroom table beside two vials of insulin. She reached for it with trembling fingers and fastened it around her wrist.

If you want to dance, you have to pay the fiddler. When Joy was in high school, that had been her mother's theme song. She'd grown sick of it. You'd think, as many times as she'd heard it, it would have sunk in.

Had payday arrived?

Struggling to control her panic, she stood at the bathroom mirror to brush her hair, and then grabbed a tissue to scrub viciously at the lipstick smeared on her pale face.

Her green eyes gazed back at her, dazed by the dilemma she'd brought on herself. No one was going to come to her rescue. She had to extricate herself.

"Why couldn't you have left well enough alone?" she asked her reflection. There were far worse things than being a little bored with your life.

Now she knew that. She had to end it without delay. Would he really talk to Larry? She tried to tell herself it was a bluff, something he'd said in a moment of anger. But she couldn't quite believe it. Graham had a streak of reckless cruelty in him.

She pinched her cheeks to force some color back into them and had a sense of suddenly falling, falling, as in a bad dream.

None of this was happening to her.

TWO

6:10 p.m.

NILA RIDGE WAITED for Graham Thornton in the empty reception room outside his office. The secretary had left more than an hour earlier. Nila's shift had ended at four, but two of the maids hadn't come to work today. She'd worked overtime to finish the cleaning, and she was determined to talk to Thornton before she went home, no matter how long she had to wait.

She wondered if her old Plymouth could get her back to town over the snow-blasted roads, then decided not to think about that now. It was a minor worry, compared with the other. She wished Thornton would come so she could get this over with.

Billy Choate, one of the waiters, had been manning the registration desk when she'd gone in search of her employer.

"Joy's taking a break," he'd said.

"I didn't see her in the dining room." Billy smirked and she asked, "Have you seen Mr. Thornton?"

"He's in his suite." This was delivered with a sly lift of Billy's eyebrows, and she understood. She couldn't go to the suite then.

Nila had suspected for weeks that something was going on between Joy and Thornton. She couldn't fathom what Joy saw in Graham Thornton, with that hunk of a husband waiting for her at home. The girl was asking for grief, but that was Joy's problem. Nila's own problems loomed so large in her mind that there was no room for anyone else's.

The seriousness of those problems made her heart race with some strange violence when she heard her employer's step in the hall.

Thornton was frowning when he entered the reception room—as though he was angry, even before he became aware of her—and the frown deepened when he saw Nila.

"What are you doing here?"

"I have to talk to you, Mr. Thornton."

"You'll get your paycheck Friday. That's your last day, isn't it?"

"Your mother said she'd speak to you."

"Mother has the flu." Nila was well aware of that. LaDonna Thornton had been home, sick, for four days now. She'd fallen ill the very afternoon she'd promised Nila to intervene with her son and urge him to reverse his decision to terminate Nila's employment as head housekeeper.

Nila had gone to LaDonna Thornton because she had nowhere else to turn. She had admitted that Graham had caught her napping. She'd been up all night with her feverish ten-year-old and was absolutely exhausted, not that she was trying to justify her laxity. It would never happen again, she'd promised.

LaDonna had understood—she was a mother herself. She knew also that Nila's husband had disappeared eight months previously, leaving her with two sons, no child support, and a mortgage, and that she desperately needed her job.

LaDonna and her son owned the lodge, although she usually left personnel decisions up to him. In Nila's case, however, she'd been sympathetic and promised to do what she could. Unfortunately, she'd been ill ever since, and Nila had not heard from her.

"She promised she'd talk to you about letting me stay on."

"She hadn't felt like dealing with trivial business details, but it wouldn't have made any difference anyway. My decision stands."

Nila twisted her small, chapped hands together nervously, trying to appear humble when what she wanted to do was slap his smug face. She was a trivial detail. "Mr. Thornton, I need this job. Please—"

He brushed her plea aside with a negligent wave of his hand. "You should have thought of that before you decided to slip off and take a nap."

"I didn't decide to—"

"You're wasting your breath, Nila. Now, if you'll excuse me." He went into his office and slammed the door.

She stared at the door and knew she was close to bursting into furious, helpless tears. What in God's name was she going to do now?

She whirled and ran from the room and down the hall, across the nearly deserted dining room, through the kitchen, where one of the cooks and a waiter looked at her curiously, and into the cubbyhole where cleaning supplies were kept. A small table and two chairs sat in the corner of the shelf-lined storeroom. Nila had been dozing at this very table when Graham Thornton slipped up to her.

She banged her fist on the table and sobbed out her rage. "Damn him . . . damn him!"

"Nila?"

Julian Moncrief, the chef, stepped out of the adjoining pantry. Nila grabbed a napkin from a dispenser and dabbed at her eyes, her back to him. Moncrief came closer. "Is there anything I can do for you?"

Gulping down tears, Nila shook her head. "Not unless you know where I can get another job by next Monday."

He patted her shoulder awkwardly. Moncrief was a tall, thin, mustachioed bachelor with an air of kingly authority. Originally from Kansas City, he'd studied in Paris and worked in several large, first-class hotels before the Thorntons hired him as chef at Eagle's Nest Lodge eighteen months ago. His aloof, superior manner kept most people at a distance.

As far as Nila could tell, his work claimed whatever passion Moncrief possessed, and he'd always seemed to her to be out of his element in this country lodge. Not surprisingly, he'd made no close friends in Buckskin, and for some reason he'd chosen Nila to be the recipient of his rare confidences.

A few weeks ago he'd told her he'd accepted the job at the lodge for health reasons. A victim of high blood pressure and peptic ulcers, he had been advised by his doctor to remove some of the stresses from his life. He'd thought the slow pace of a rural setting would be exactly what the doctor ordered. Perhaps it was, but after eighteen months he was giving himself another ulcer, chafing under the "limitations" of his current employment. He'd confided to Nila last week that he'd applied for the head chef's position at a large new Dallas hotel.

He tugged on his luxuriant mustache. "You talked to Thornton?"

She closed her eyes briefly, seeing the irritable flip of Thornton's hand, as though she were of no more importance than a pesky gnat, hearing the rude slam of his office door. She was already five months behind in her mortgage payments. Two months ago, the savings and loan had agreed to give her a reasonable amount of time to catch up, but what did they consider reasonable? If they knew she'd lost her job...

"I tried. He wouldn't listen." She balled the paper napkin in her fist. "He said I was wasting my breath. I wanted to kill him! I don't know what I'm going to do, Julian."

"You'll find something."

She whirled on him. "What?" she asked bitterly. "I'm not trained in a good-paying profession, like you. Do you know how lucky you are to be getting that job in Dallas?"

"Haven't you heard? I'm out of the running." The corners of his mouth turned down and his mustache drooped. "Thornton made sure of that."

He was a foot taller than her petite five feet, and she tilted her head back to see him better. Hate hardened his usually remote eyes. She understood exactly what he was feeling.

"What did he do?"

"Gave me a bad reference. An insult. A slap in the face." He tweaked his mustache angrily. "Apparently there's no limit to how low the man will stoop to get what he wants."

"I can't imagine what he could find to criticize in your performance."

"He *couldn't* find anything, of course. He had to fabricate something. He told them I drink on the job, that I'm not reliable."

She'd never known Julian to touch anything stronger than ginger ale while working. "Why would he lie?"

With a quick toss of his head, he swept a deep wave of mud-brown hair out of eyes that still glittered dangerously. "To keep me from leaving," he snapped, as though it should have been obvious.

Abandoning the bushy growth of hair on his upper lip, he gripped the back of a chair with both hands, turning his long, elegant fingers white. "He's not likely to find someone of my caliber to replace me." He threw a glance toward the kitchen, his lip curling contemptuously. "A chef must be constantly challenged to keep from going stale. Most of the guests in this establishment think fettuccine is a Mafia don. Forget that there's nowhere to go after work. I need the excitement of a city and a big hotel. If I don't get out of here soon, they'll have to cart me off in a straitjacket."

"I'm sorry," Nila said. She did feel sympathy for Julian, but his situation wasn't nearly as desperate as hers; he still had a job. "Maybe you can convince the people in Dallas that Thornton lied to keep you here."

"I doubt it. No, the Dallas job's lost."

"Oh, Julian, you should at least try—"

"I won't beg! Never mind. I'll find another position, and next time I won't give Thornton a chance to stab me in the back."

"But they'll insist on references. How will you get around that?"

"I don't know." His mouth twisted grimly. "I'll think of something."

THREE

A DARK-SHROUDED FIGURE left the lodge by an exit at the end of the south wing. The heavy door swung closed behind the figure, the lock engaging with a sharp click.

The snow had been falling for nearly three hours, blanketing the ground, softening the contours of shrubs and trees. Hiding secret comings and goings. It seemed to cover the last few minutes with an eerie unreality, as though it might never have happened.

The dark figure clung to the blank stone wall of the lodge and peered through the driving curtain of snow, seeing only the suggestion of an endless whiteness.

No one within that limited range of vision. Good. Couldn't afford to be seen near this exit. Whether it was possible to enter and leave the suite without being seen had been the big question mark in the plan. The blizzard was fortuitous.

With gloved hands the figure pulled the dark collar closer. A painful twist of fear flamed for an instant, then was replaced by righteous anger. He had left no other option. When you back somebody into a corner, you must expect desperate reactions.

The anger was quickly snuffed out. The door was locked. There was no going back. It was done. Over.

The figure moved quickly through the veil of snow into the darkness, leaving footprints that were soon obliterated.

NEAR BY, A WATCHER crouched behind a snow-blanketed bush, attention caught by the dark-shrouded figure's stealthy haste. There was something familiar about the way the figure moved. A sense of near-recognition flickered for an instant, then went out. Something to think about later, when graver concerns did not glut the mind. Such flashes of déjà vu usually came back in clearer outline, given enough time.

FOUR

9:30 p.m.

THE SNOW WAS an endless slanting white curtain blowing against the pickup windshield. Lucille Hummingbird had left home, a small acreage on Highway 10 west of Buckskin, at nine fifteen, allowing forty-five minutes for the drive to Eagle's Nest Lodge on an arm of Lake Tenkiller, east of town, a trip she ordinarily made in fifteen minutes.

Henry had urged her to stay at home tonight. But she was the only one on the front desk from ten P.M. until six A.M., and if she didn't go, either Joy Yeaky would be pressed to work a double shift or Mr. Thornton himself would have to cover the desk, which wouldn't endear her to her quick-tempered employer. A week ago he'd caught Nila Ridge napping on the job and fired her on the spot. Most employers would have given her a warning and a second chance but not Thornton.

Lucille doubted he'd consider the snow a valid reason for missing work, especially not now when the staff was gearing up for an influx of guests for the week ending with the lodge's "first annual" New Year's Eve ball.

The week between Christmas and New Year's was to be the high point of the winter season, and Thornton had advertised extensively in a four-state area. The advertising had paid off; the lodge was booked solid for the last week of the year.

As the pickup crept cautiously through the dense snow, Lucille leaned as far forward as the seat belt would allow, straining to see the road. It was impossible to tell if she was still right of center. She prayed she wouldn't meet another car before she turned off for the lodge. She was beginning to wish she'd risked Thornton's wrath and stayed at home.

She disliked working nights, even if it was the only sensible arrangement. If she worked days, she would have to turn over most of her take-home pay to a babysitter. As it was, Henry was with their three children while she was at work and vice versa.

Since she'd taken the job at the lodge, they'd doubled up on the pickup payments. Next spring, when the pickup was paid off, they could do some work on the house. It was badly in need of painting inside and out, and the living room carpet should have been replaced before two-year-old Jill was born. Maybe they could even squeeze a new dishwasher into the budget to replace the one that hadn't been in working order for months.

Lucille cleared a circle in the windshield fog with her gloved hand; the defroster didn't seem to be working as it should. Was that a car ahead? She squinted, trying to bring the faint, hazy blobs into focus. A snow-covered mound approached her through the swirling whiteness. It seemed to Lucille to be coming at a dangerously reckless clip. The driver laid on the horn. The sudden harsh blare made her heart lurch. Reflexively, Lucille jerked the wheel sharply to the right. Where *was* the road?

Suddenly, in front of her, the lodge sign loomed, ice sculpted, high on its pole. She swung wide to the right for the turnoff as the oncoming car ground past, horn still blaring.

"All *right!*" Lucille muttered. "I hear you." And then the pickup started to slide.

She fought the wheel. Later she couldn't recall whether she'd turned into the slide, as Henry had instructed, or away from it. It happened too fast for thought. Whatever she did, it had no effect on the pickup, which headed with a sickening rush for the shoulder and the steep bar ditch. With an awful clarity, Lucille saw the ditch rising to meet her and beyond the ditch the shore of the lake. As the truck slithered sideways and plowed down the incline, her full weight pitched forward against the seat belt.

The truck came to rest, nose down, with a bone-jarring thud that whipped her head back against the seat. She sat in the dead silence that followed, her gloved hands still gripping the wheel. The truck had stopped short of the lake, and she was conscious and in no great pain. When this awareness was communicated to her body, her heartbeat slowed and she released the wheel and turned off the headlights, removed the key from the ignition. Her hands were shaking.

She worked her fingers a few times, then took several deep, steadying breaths. Merciful God, what a close call. No job was worth taking such a risk.

The pickup had gone as far as it was going tonight. It would take a wrecker to get the truck back on the road again. She released her seat belt and worked arms and legs, then her neck, which already felt a little sore. Reassured that nothing was broken, she got out of the truck, hanging on to the door until she was on firm footing.

Fortunately, she'd worn wool slacks and heavy rubber boots over her low-heeled shoes. She pulled up the hood of her down jacket, tying the cord beneath her chin.

The lights of the lodge were dim and distant. She trudged along the ditch, her boots sinking through deep drifts. The ground began to rise, the ditch growing progressively more shallow, until she could maneuver the slope and climb back to the lane. She stood there for a moment, catching her breath. Viewed through the thick-falling snow, the lodge appeared much farther away than a mere quarter mile.

If she fell and injured herself, she probably wouldn't be found until morning. Even if she called for help, she wasn't likely to be heard.

Stop it, Lucille.

Of course she'd be found before morning. If she didn't show up for work, someone would call her house and Henry would come looking for her. Besides, she wasn't going to fall.

She listened to the crunch of her boots and thought about the warmth and light awaiting her at the lodge. Perhaps there would be time enough before her shift started to go to the kitchen and make a cup of hot chocolate.

She kept her eyes on the lights. The snow made them appear to flicker erratically, but she must have walked halfway already. In a few minutes, she'd be safe and snug inside.

A blood-curdling scream rent the night. Like the sound of a woman being tortured.

Lucille tried to run, slipped, went down on one knee and somehow recovered her balance before she realized what she'd heard. A screech owl. It must be in one of the trees near the lodge.

She had a premonition of disaster.

Something terrible is going to happen. The words formed in Lucille's mind, as clear as a voice from heaven. This was the third night in a row that a screech owl had been heard near the lodge. Billy Choate, a waiter at the lodge, had been agitated last night because he had heard the owl for the second time. Lucille had tried to reason him out of his anxiety, but Billy was a true believer in Cherokee witches, night walkers.

As had been Lucille's Grandmother Drum. The old woman had filled Lucille's childhood years with the stories told by the old people of the tribe. Children were warned not to go out alone at night, lest they meet an evil night walker. In all likelihood, if that should happen, they wouldn't recognize the witch until it was too late, for witches often assumed the form of an animal or a bird. A screech owl was a favorite disguise. If one heard a screech owl three nights in succession, it was almost certain to be a night walker seeking to further his evil designs.

Lucille had never told her own children the tales that had terrorized her childhood. She had closed a door on them, determined that, in her family, the cycle would stop with her generation. All very sensible, as far as it went; but let a screech owl's shriek rip the fabric of a still night and frightful images would bob to the surface of her mind, as though they'd been waiting for the opportunity.

Her heart thudded with a trepidation that amazed her. She found herself wishing fervently that she had never set foot out of her house tonight, not so much

because the pickup was nose down in a ditch but so that
she would not have been gripped by this sick, shaking
fear.

She hadn't believed in Grandmother Drum's superstitions for years. She had put the old lady's beliefs
down to ignorance. But just now the usually firm
ground of her rational convictions was too shaky to
hold her, and a scream clawed its way up into her
throat. She choked it down, unvoiced. But she could
not choke off her thoughts.

Grandmother Drum, who had died only two months
ago, had warned Lucille not to take the job at the lodge
because, she said, it was built on the site of an old Indian cemetery. Rumors that the lodge sat on an Indian
graveyard had persisted ever since construction plans
were made public. But there hadn't been a single grave
marker in the area, and the construction workers found
no human remains when the foundation footings were
dug.

Nonetheless, Grandmother Drum insisted that as a
child she had seen in that spot several little wood
houses with roofs made of hand-hewn shingles, which
earlier generations of Cherokees had built at the heads
of graves. The little houses had rotted away long ago,
the old lady said, but the graves remained.

Privately, Lucille had considered Grandmother
Drum senile. The workers had found no graves on the
site. It was doubtful there had ever been a cemetery in
that location. Even if there had been two or three
graves there long ago, all evidence of them had disin-
tegrated.

That aside, spirits did not rise from graves to haunt
those who had the audacity to build on their burial
sites. Lucille knew all of this with her rational mind,

but at the moment, in this strange white wasteland, with the wind howling low like a nervous beast and the wind-driven snow stinging her face, her grandmother's warning was a silent shriek of panic in her ears.

The hairs on the back of her head stirred eerily. Suddenly she realized that her hands were sweating under the gloves, and, in spite of the cold that seemed to penetrate her jacket, a tiny thread of sweat worked its way between her breasts.

Against all reason, a conviction that she was being followed gripped her. She whirled to peer over her shoulder.

Cold stung her eyes and made them water. She raised her hand, rubbed her eyes, squinted again. She could see nothing. The whole world was a white void.

Nervously, she sighed, and, head bowed against the wind, she struggled up the rising ground toward the lodge. Snow had edged over the tops of her boots, and when she moved now her feet squished in soggy socks.

She watched the lodge come closer. It was built of limestone and rough-cut cedar, a three-story, dome-shaped center section with long, two-story wings extending out on opposite sides. It had always reminded Lucille of a huge octopus with only two tentacles.

At last she had crossed the front parking area and reached the wide steps leading to the lodge entrance. Someone had cleared the snow from the steps earlier, but another two or three inches had fallen since then.

Lucille's sense of oncoming disaster remained strong. Now that the heavy, carved door of the lodge was within reach, she could tell herself her premonition had nothing to do with the screech owl; it was formless and vague, but, in spite of that, it felt quite real.

She reminded herself that feelings could be far removed from reality.

She trudged up the steps and pulled open the big door. She stepped inside and sagged for a moment against it, letting the warmth seep through her clothing.

She looked around her at the flagstone floor and beyond that to the thick brown carpeting, the high, steep-pitched, beamed ceiling, the rough-cedar-paneled walls, the massive panes of glass holding back the void.

In an instant, her perceptions shifted to form a new pattern, like a drawing for children in which several animals are hidden. If you stared at the drawing long enough, you would eventually see all the animals. From inside, Lucille saw the environment from a different perspective. She had stepped from a threatening, alien world into one that was familiar and welcoming.

What had come over her out there? She'd nearly lost control of herself as well as the pickup. Imagine taking her grandmother's superstitions seriously and being frightened into a panic by a screech owl. Hysteria. What she needed was a cup of something hot, and she'd be her normal, sensible self again.

Then she saw Billy Choate hurrying toward her, his bronze face a mask of fear.

"Did you hear it?"

Lucille did not have to ask what he meant. "Yes. It must have a nest near the lodge. It's only an owl, Billy." What a hypocrite I am, Lucille thought. She smiled, intending to reassure him. "I have ten minutes before I'm due at the desk. Let's go to the kitchen and make hot chocolate."

Walking beside her, Billy gestured with his thumb toward the night beyond the glass. Leaning down, he spoke in low tones. "Were you able to see it?"

He was a gangly twenty-year-old with a few chin hairs for a beard, which he disposed of with tweezers. Henry always said one of the best things about being an Indian man was that you didn't have to shave every day.

At the moment, Billy's dark, hairless face was as rigid as a mask, as though the bones and muscles had turned to concrete beneath the skin. Fear emanated from him in waves.

"I couldn't even see the tree, Billy," she said quietly, hoping that soft, slow speech would have an calming effect. "But I know a screech owl when I hear one."

"Then you must have thought about what it could mean."

Lucille kept a poker face. "I thought the poor thing must be as cold as a well digger's butt, sitting up in that tree. I suppose feathers are good insulation, though."

She pushed through the kitchen door, Billy at her heels, and hit the light switch just inside. A row of fluorescent bulbs down the center of the room blinked on. The cold gleam of stainless steel made Lucille think of a hospital laboratory. She took off her boots and jacket and stowed them in a closet off the kitchen. She removed her wet socks and hung them over the closet rod. Her bare feet felt cold and clammy in the leather loafers.

When she returned to the kitchen, Billy, still in his white waiter's coat, stood uncertainly in the center of the room, where she'd left him.

"You get the milk," Lucille said, "while I find a saucepan and the cocoa mix."

Billy looked at her a moment longer, dark eyes wary under protuberant brows. He sighed. "Okay."

While the milk heated, Lucille spooned cocoa mix into two mugs. Billy sat down at the table where kitchen employees took their breaks and put his head in his hands. Lucille added a few marshmallows to the mugs and brought them to the table.

She squeezed Billy's shoulder. "Drink. You'll feel better."

He looked up at her. "I don't believe you didn't think of a night walker when you heard the owl."

Sitting down, she cradled her mug in both hands. "Of course I thought of it, Billy. I was raised on ghost stories, the same as you. That doesn't mean I believe them."

"I've seen too many weird things happen, things that can't be explained."

"Things *you* can't explain, you mean. That's not to say somebody somewhere couldn't explain them."

He shook his head.

"Come on, Billy, you're scaring yourself with those old superstitions."

He shrugged stoically. "I can't go out there. I'll stay here tonight."

She frowned. "Where?"

"I'll find someplace to stretch out. I probably won't be able to sleep anyway. If Thornton finds out, I'll say I didn't want to drive in the storm."

"It's not a bad idea," she said finally. "My pickup slid into a ditch just this side of the turnoff. I'll have to get a wrecker out here in the morning."

Billy stared at her. "You *walked* from the high-way?"

"A mere quarter mile." She wanted to forget that seemingly endless walk when she'd discovered that the old fears had not been banished after all. Instead, they lurked in a corner of her brain in the mire of dark, childish memories.

"That's not what I mean."

"I know. Look, I'm here, aren't I? Safe and sound."

"Maybe you're not the one it's after."

Impossible to reason him out of his obsession. "Why don't you come out to the desk and talk to me for a while. You can use one of the sofas in the lobby when you're ready to turn in. Surely there won't be any late check-ins on a night like this. I have to go and relieve Joy now."

"She should stay here till morning."

"Not a word about the screech owl, Billy. Promise me."

He nodded. "But she shouldn't be driving."

"Bring your chocolate," Lucille said.

Joy Yeaky was already dressed in her coat and fur-lined boots. When she saw Lucille and Billy, she took a blue wool scarf from her pocket and wound it around her blond head. She was a pretty young woman with a gamine face and dark-lashed green eyes in drastic con-trast to milk-pale skin.

"I was worried that you weren't coming," Joy said to Lucille. "I must have been in the ladies' when you got here."

"I had to walk from the highway," Lucille said. "I lost control of my truck."

Joy's green eyes widened. "Are you all right?"

"I'll be sore tomorrow, but I'm fine."

"We don't think you should drive tonight," Billy said, looking to Lucille for confirmation.

"The road is treacherous," Lucille agreed.

"A pickup's the last thing you want to drive on icy roads," Joy said matter-of-factly. She reached behind the registration desk for her purse. "Not enough weight in the rear. My Bronco has four-wheel drive and snow tires. I could climb the side of a mountain if I had to. Need a ride to town, Billy?"

"Uh, no... I'm not going yet, and neither should you."

"I'll chance it." She lifted a gloved hand and wiggled her fingers at them. "Larry will be waiting up for me." She frowned as though the thought of her husband waiting worried her. Lucille hoped things were all right with Joy and Larry. In recent weeks, Joy had seemed restless, even worried, and Lucille had wondered if the young couple were having problems. But she didn't feel she knew Joy well enough to ask.

"Night," Joy said as she walked across the lobby to the door leading to the employees' parking lot in back.

"Joy," Lucille called after her, "call me when you get home. If I don't hear from you, I'll give Larry a ring."

"I'll do it."

Lucille swallowed the last of her hot chocolate and set the mug on the desk. Billy seemed to notice that he still held his own mug and set it beside Lucille's. He walked over to one of the big panes and peered out. Lucille went to stand beside him.

"She'll be all right, Billy."

The parking lot was well lit. They watched Joy pick her way through a deep drift toward her Bronco.

"Look at that," Billy said sharply.

Odd. The driver's door was standing open. Joy stopped short, seeing the open door for the first time. She hesitated, then went ahead, halting to brush piled-up snow off the windshield. Lucille envied her, going home to her husband and a warm bed.

Joy walked around the open driver's door. Then, instead of getting in, she staggered back a few steps. She stood there for a moment, looking into the car, as though she were frozen to the spot.

Lucille felt Billy stiffen beside her. "What's wrong? Why doesn't she get in?"

"Maybe the seat's full of snow."

Joy screamed. The high-pitched wail sent a cold stab of fear through Lucille. Her first, flashing thought was that it sounded amazingly like the screech owl's, as though it were an echo of doom.

Then Joy stumbled back toward the lodge. Her Cupid's bow mouth worked grotesquely and her green eyes stared in shock. Lucille couldn't hear what she was saying, but as Joy came closer she read her lips.

"No, no!" Joy was moaning. "Oh, my God, no..."

FIVE

10:30 p.m.

"IT'S LATE, and the weather's too bad to go out again tonight." Buckskin police chief Mitchell Bushyhead looked up from his easy chair at his fifteen-year-old daughter. She'd barely said three words to him since he came home at six thirty. All his attempts at conversation had bounced off her. She'd gone directly to her room after dinner and hadn't come out again until now, though he'd heard her on the telephone several times. Evidently the latest phone conversation had been with her best friend, Temple Roberts.

Emily was dressed in the clothes she'd worn to school that morning: faded jeans—stone washed, he thought they were called—a red sweater, and mid-thigh-high brown leather boots. He'd expected her to be in her pajamas and robe long ago, but his usually amiable daughter had not been behaving in the expected manner today.

"You slept over at the Robertses' Saturday night, remember. You'll wear out your welcome."

She tucked a strand of long brown hair behind her ear and crossed her arms over her breasts. "Temple wouldn't have asked me if I weren't welcome."

"Tomorrow's a school day."

She didn't move, didn't respond.

"No homework?"

"No."

"Then how about a game of Scrabble?"

She rolled her eyes. "Oh, Daddy."

Sunday night, when they'd decorated the Christmas tree, she'd seemed fine. The next afternoon, it was as if another girl had moved into the house, one who had an aversion to being in the same room with Mitch. The tree they'd decorated together sat in a corner of the living room. The merry blink of its lights seemed to mock him.

"I'm sorry, but it's foolhardy to go out on a night like this when you don't have to."

"The snow's no problem for the Land Cruiser. I thought that's why you bought it, for bad roads."

It was true he'd used that reasoning to justify buying the four-wheel drive vehicle. It handled terrain that would have defeated his old Buick. But mainly the Land Cruiser appealed to the boy in him. Since he'd bought it a month ago, he'd spent several hundred dollars rigging it up with a front-bumper winch, a heavy-duty trailer hitch (in preparation for the day he could afford a bass boat), and fog, spot, and backup lights.

Lisa called it his new toy. "All you need now," she'd teased, "is a foxtail for your aerial and a horn that plays chimes."

Emily jammed her fingers into the tight pockets of her jeans and released an exaggerated sigh. He hated to see her unhappy, so he relented a little. After all, it was only a few blocks to the Robertses' house. "Okay, if you can't stand my company, ask Temple to come over here tonight. We'll go pick her up."

She tossed her hair back. "I don't want to stay here." She turned on her heel and started for the stairs, mumbling, "I'd think you'd be glad to get rid of me so you wouldn't have to stay here, either."

The Christmas-tree lights winked at him as he tossed his newspaper to the floor and rose to his feet. "Emily!"

She halted stiffly at the foot of the stairs. "What do you want?"

"You can turn around and face me, for starters."

Reluctantly, she did so.

"Now, what did you mean by that last remark?"

She lifted her shoulders. "Don't you know?"

"If I knew, I wouldn't have to ask."

She glared at him. "You don't really care what I say or think."

About when he thought he understood his daughter, she came out with something totally nonsensical. He knew that fifteen was a difficult age, especially if you'd lost your mother in the past year. It hadn't been an easy transition for either of them, but he thought they'd worked through the worst of it. Emily had many friends, and she'd been involved in numerous extracurricular activities since school started—being on the pom-pom squad and in the all-school play, helping build a float for the Homecoming Parade, taking driver's ed, going on her first real dates with Kevin Hartsbarger.

Wait a minute...maybe she and Kevin were quits. Not exactly a tragedy from her father's viewpoint, but to a fifteen-year-old girl, breaking up with a boyfriend could seem like the end of the world.

He felt woefully inadequate to advise his daughter in matters of the heart. At times like this, he missed Ellen so much he felt sick. She and Emily had been very close.... "Honey, if you'd like to talk...about anything."

"Why should I? You won't talk to *me*!"

More nonsense. "Would you mind translating that? I've been trying to talk to you all day, and getting nowhere."

"I mean you don't talk to me about anything important," she flared. "You have this whole secret life that I don't know anything about. I have to hear from other people what's going on with you—where you go when I'm not here, like Saturday night when I was at the Robertses'."

Secret life? Oh, shit. It dawned on Mitch, what she had stuck in her craw. She'd heard about Lisa. Someone must have seen him going into Lisa's garage apartment Saturday night. Or maybe they'd noticed his Toyota parked at the curb until nearly dawn. Word had traveled on the grapevine to Emily.

He should have talked to her about Lisa before this. He'd meant to, but he'd been waiting for the right moment. Mitch had been seeing Lisa Macpherson for three months now, and he still hadn't found an appropriate time to face Emily with it. He hadn't wanted to make waves when things were going so well between them. He'd feared she'd react exactly as she was reacting, with outrage and a sense of betrayal.

He couldn't blame Emily for her feelings. She had a right to expect honesty from her father. He'd been stupid to think he could keep a secret like that in Buckskin until he worked up the courage to tell Emily.

"You're right. I should have told you about Lisa."

She said nothing.

"So you know where I went Saturday night."

Her brown eyes flashed. "You were in Lisa Macpherson's apartment! All night!"

It was as bad as he'd feared. "Now, wait a minute—not all night."

"How could you, Daddy?" Tears filled her eyes, and she wiped them angrily on the sleeve of her sweater. "How could you be so...so disloyal to Mother's memory? She hasn't even been dead a year!"

He felt her pain and his throat thickened. He went to her and caressed her hair. "I'm not being disloyal, sweetheart. I'll always love your mother, you know that. I miss her as much as you do. But life has to go on, you and I have to go on." He winced inwardly. Why couldn't he express his deepest feelings without falling back on clichés?

Emily shrugged his hand away. "Obviously Mrs. Macpherson is helping you *go on*. I can't believe I have to sit in English class and look at her five days a week!"

"Emily, you're not even trying to understand."

She stiffened. "She'll never take my mother's place!"

He raked a hand through his black hair. "Nobody can do that. Honey, it's no big deal. Lisa and I have seen each other a few times. We're friends. There's a long way from thinking about any kind of commitment."

She clapped her hands over her ears. "I don't want to hear about her. Just leave me alone." She whirled and started up the stairs.

The telephone rang. Mitch uttered an oath. "Emily, we have to talk about this." Her bedroom door slammed as he strode to the kitchen and snatched the receiver off its hook. "Hello!" he bellowed.

"Mitch, we've got a body."

It was Virgil Rabbit, the oldest of the three police officers who worked under Mitch, and Mitch's closest friend. Virgil covered the four-to-midnight shift. "Your timing stinks, Virgil."

"Well, excuse me all to hell. The stiff didn't ask me when would be a convenient time to die. If he had, I sure wouldn't have suggested tonight."

"Car wreck?"

"I don't think so. One of the employees out at the lodge found a body in her car. That's all I know. Billy Choate called the station. He wasn't very coherent. I tried to find out if he knew the dead man, but he hung up on me. Could you swing by here in your Land Cruiser and pick me up? I'm afraid to try to make it out there in the patrol car."

Mitch muttered an expletive. He'd voted against bringing the lake community east of town into Buckskin's city limits, preferring to leave it in the county sheriff's jurisdiction. But, in spite of his and a few other people's vocal opposition, they'd been outvoted.

Oscar Thornton, the wealthy real estate developer who built the lodge and dropped dead of a heart attack days before it opened, had launched an effective campaign to bring the voters over to his side, playing up the new jobs the lodge would create and promising to fill them with local people whenever possible. He'd wanted access to the town's water and its fire department.

Now Mitch was forced to handle an enlarged territory encompassing several hundred new residents, without additional personnel. He'd complained to the city council so often, they had promised to find the money for another officer, but they hadn't as yet made good on their word.

"I'd better see if Doc Sullivan can go with us," Mitch said. Dr. Sullivan would stand in for the medical examiner until the official M.E. could get to Buckskin from Tahlequah. With the storm, that probably wouldn't be until late tomorrow. "I'll be there as fast as I can, Virgil."

He climbed the stairs and knocked on Emily's door. "I have to go out on police business. Do you want me to ask Mrs. Morgan to come over and stay with you?" Their next-door neighbor came in twice a month to clean, and she'd stayed overnight with Emily once with Mitch had to be out of town.

"No." The reply was muffled.

"I might be gone for quite a while. There's been a death out at the lodge."

"Mmmm."

"If you change your mind, call Mrs. Morgan. If you're asleep when I get back, we'll talk in the morning."

There was no answer.

EMILY LAY ON HER BED, her face buried in her pillow. Until a few minutes ago, she'd clung to the slim hope that the rumor she'd heard was false. She felt betrayed. By Lisa Macpherson as well as her father. The English teacher sponsored the pom-pom squad, and Emily had spent more time with her this term than with any of her other teachers. She'd really liked her. But there had been several opportunities, when nobody else was around, for Lisa to tell Emily that she was seeing her father, and she'd said nothing.

When Rick Farmer, who sat behind Emily in geometry class, had told her he'd seen her father's car at Lisa Macpherson's apartment, she'd tried to pretend it didn't matter. "So?" she'd said, and Rick had snickered into his hand. It did matter, though. So much that she'd almost convinced herself Rick had mistaken somebody else's Land Cruiser for her father's. Dumb. There was no other gray Land Cruiser in Buckskin. She'd known what her father was doing there, but still she hadn't released that little sliver of hope that he'd have another explanation. Dumber still. What other explanation could there be for being at Lisa Macpherson's apartment so late at night?

She turned over on her back and stared at the ceiling. How long had it been going on? Her father said they'd seen each other a few times, but what did "a few" mean? Twice? Ten times? And did it really make that much difference? She thought that once would hurt her as much as a dozen. It was the principle involved. How could her father *look* at another woman after living with her adored mother for sixteen years?

The telephone beside the bed rang and made her jump. She wasn't used to having the extension in her room. Her father had had it installed last week, saying it was an early Christmas present. Now she wondered if the white slim-line extension was salve for a guilty conscience. She reached for the receiver.

"Hello."

"Hi, Emmy."

He was the only person in the world who called her Emmy. "Hullo, Kevin."

"You sound down. You okay?"

"Terrific. What have you been doing?"

"Studying for my chemistry midterm, what else? That class is eating my lunch. Are you ready for all your tests?"

"Yes, at least I've decided I've studied enough. Whatever will be will be."

"You sure you're okay?"

"I'll live."

"Well, don't get too excited about it."

She tried to laugh, but it didn't work.

"Guess what?" he asked.

"I give up."

"My cousin Dirk from Tahlequah is coming over for the weekend."

"The baseball player you're always talking about?"

"Yeah, and I had an idea. Do you think we could fix him up with Temple Friday night? We could double."

"I'll ask her. I can probably talk her into it. He'd better not be a jerk, though."

"Trust me." She giggled weakly, and he asked, "Have you talked to your father about Mrs. Macpherson yet?"

"Sort of."

"And?"

She drew in a deep breath in an effort to dislodge the weight on her chest. "He didn't even try to deny it. He acted like I should have expected it. Life goes on and all that crap, you know?"

"Uh—well, Emmy, maybe he's right. You are being kind of tough on him."

It was easy for Kevin to talk. His father wasn't seeing a woman who wasn't his mother. "I thought I could at least depend on you and Temple to understand," she said stiffly.

"I do understand, Emmy, but I can kind of see your father's side, too."

Perhaps he was the wrong sex to empathize with her. Men were different from women. Emily felt sure that, if it had been her father who died, her mother would have remained single and celibate for years. "Well, maybe you'll draw me a picture sometime," she said, stiffer yet.

"Hey, don't take it out on me. I didn't introduce them."

"Oh, I know. I'm sorry."

"Want me to pick you up for school in the morning—if I can get out of my driveway?"

"If you want to."

"Okay. You'll talk to Temple, then?"

"I said I would."

He sighed. "Right. See you later."

"Bye, Kevin." She hung up and stared at the ceiling some more. The lump in her throat seemed to get bigger.

A PAUNCHY GUARD who looked to be in his sixties came out of the security booth as the Land Cruiser approached. Mitch opened the car window a crack.

"About time you got here," the guard shouted next to Mitch's ear. "Got a near panic on my hands. That little gal who found the body came unglued." He nodded vigorously, agreeing with himself. "Nearly tossed my cookies myself. He's sure 'nough froze stiff and agrinnin'." He swung his arm. "Pull 'er on around back. He's in the Bronco."

Few lights could be seen in the lodge's guest room windows. Occupancy probably was down at this time of year, Mitch guessed, and most of the guests who were in residence had evidently turned in early. Not much else to do on a night like this.

"At least the snow seems to be letting up a little," Mitch said as he pulled in beside the snow-covered shape of a four-wheel-drive vehicle. The driver's door stood open.

Doc Sullivan tugged an orange hunter's cap with fur-lined ear flaps down over his gray hair and grabbed his clipboard. Mitch pulled up the hood of the sweatshirt he wore beneath his coat. The three men got out of the Land Cruiser.

"Damn," Virgil muttered. "Left my cap in my other coat." He hunched his shoulders in his tan down jacket, trying to raise them far enough to protect his bare ears. "Billy said they left everything the way they found it."

Mitch's most experienced officer, Virgil was forty-one years old, a full-blood Cherokee. He carried a camera with a flash attachment for recording the scene. Death would probably turn out to have resulted from natural causes or an accident. Maybe the dead man had been drunk, passed out, and died of exposure. But they'd have the pictures on file if questions arose later.

"I guess she did panic, like the guard said," Sullivan observed. "Left the door open. Think it'll start?"

"The dome light's still on," Mitch pointed out.

"I think she left the door open because that's the way she found it," Virgil said. "Leastways, that's what Billy Choate said."

They stepped calf-deep in snow as they approached the Bronco's open door. The corpse, wearing an over-coat and cowboy boots, lay sprawled half on, half off, the front seat. The head and hands were bare. One hand clutched the neck, as though the man had been tearing at his throat when he died. Mitch took all of this in with a glance that then settled on the face. The eyes were open, and the mouth was twisted and agape in an ugly death rictus.

Sullivan sucked in a breath. "Good Lord, it's Graham Thornton."

Mitch had already recognized the man. The Thorntons, Oscar and LaDonna, their college-age daughter, Cara, and son, Graham, with his wife, Magda, had moved into the lake community near the lodge two years previously. After Oscar's death, Graham and his mother had assumed management of the lodge. Mitch didn't know much about the family. Except for the campaign preceding the election incorporating the area into the town, they hadn't involved themselves in Buckskin activities.

Sullivan leaned across the car seat and pressed his fingers against Thornton's neck below the jaw, feeling for a pulse that all three men knew wasn't there. He drew his hand away from the corpse and straightened, shaking his head. "He's long gone."

"Doesn't heart trouble run in families, Doc?" Virgil asked.

Sullivan stomped his fast-numbing feet and frowned. "Genetics is a factor, but Graham was only thirty-four. He was a diabetic. Diagnosed when he was sixteen. Otherwise, he was seemingly in excellent health. He's been under my care since he moved here, and there've never been any abnormalities in his EKGs."

"Maybe there was a complication from the diabetes," Mitch suggested.

"Maybe," Sullivan said, "but he was a very well-controlled diabetic. Stayed on the prescribed exercise program and stuck to his diet and injections religiously. He's never had a problem with it since I've been seeing him.''

"Guess we'll have to wait for the autopsy," Mitch said. "Anything else you want to do here, Doc?"

Sullivan shook his head. "Let's call an ambulance."

"Get a few pictures, Virgil, and then join Doc and me in the lodge. We'll see what we can learn from the employees."

Inside, Sullivan went straight to a phone to call for the ambulance. A young Indian man and two women, one a short, compact Cherokee about thirty years old, the other a younger white woman, sat close together on a sofa, as though for warmth. The man wore a white waiter's jacket. The older woman had close-cropped hair and was dressed in a gray sweater and wool slacks. She looked like the type of female who had been a tomboy while growing up.

The younger woman, who was thin and quite pretty, wore a white blouse, jade-green corduroy skirt, and black fur-lined boots. A dark wine coat was folded over a chair near the blonde. Mitch knew Lucille Hummingbird and Billy Choate, though not well. He thought the blonde was young Larry Yeaky's wife.

Sullivan finished his call and, sitting down, began filling in parts of a death-certificate form attached to his clipboard. Mitch approached the three huddled on the couch.

"Hello, Lucille, Billy. And it's Mrs. Yeaky, isn't it?"

The blonde nodded. "Joy—Joy Yeaky."

"Who found the body?"

Joy Yeaky swallowed hard before she whispered, "I did. My shift ended at ten. I went out to my Bronco to go home and—the door was open. When I looked in..." Her hand fluttered upward, then settled back in her lap to pluck at the corduroy fabric of her skirt, as though trying to express what her mouth couldn't put into words.

Lucille Hummingbird stilled the young woman's restless hand by covering it with her own in a maternal gesture. "She was sure Mr. Thornton was dead, but I went out and double-checked," Lucille said. "He was gone."

Mitch pulled over an armchair, turning it to face the sofa, and sat down. Joy Yeaky's green eyes met Mitch's gaze for an instant, then darted away. "Do you know why he was in your car?"

She shook her head vehemently. "I saw him leave the lodge earlier—about seven forty-five, I think. I work at the registration desk, and he came through the lobby. He said he'd be at his mother's house, if we needed him. Mrs. Thornton has been sick, and Graham—Mr. Thornton—wanted to check on her."

"He didn't say anything about borrowing your Bronco?"

"No, he wouldn't have done that. He might not've been back by the time my shift ended."

"The lodge has a four-wheel-drive Jeep," Billy interjected. "It's in a garage north of the lodge. Mr. Thornton would've used that, unless he planned to walk. Mrs. Thornton's house is just down the road, less than a half mile from here."

As Billy talked, Mitch noticed an abnormal rigidity in his features. His mouth barely moved, as though his face were nearly paralyzed. Mitch also noticed that he kept shooting worried glances at the bank of windows overlooking the parking lot where the Bronco sat. He's terrified, Mitch realized. Did Billy know something about Thornton's death?

"Did you see Mr. Thornton leave the lodge?" Mitch asked Billy.

Billy looked at Joy as though in apology. "No, I worked in the dining room until after it closed. We stop admitting diners at nine on weeknights."

"What about you, Lucille? Did you see Mr. Thornton leave the lodge?"

"Oh, no. I work nights at the registration desk. I didn't get here until a little before ten."

"You relieve Joy?"

Lucille nodded. "When I got here, Billy and I went to the kitchen for hot chocolate. We both came out here at ten so Joy could leave."

Dr. Sullivan had finished writing and was listening attentively to Mitch's interrogation.

"I'd decided to bed down here tonight," Billy said. "We tried to get Joy to stay, too. Lucille's pickup was already in a ditch, and we were afraid the same thing would happen to Joy. But she insisted on leaving."

"I knew I could get to town in the Bronco," Joy said defensively. "I—I wish I'd stayed inside, though. Oh—" She covered her face with her hands and mumbled. "He looked so—so horrible."

Virgil came into the foyer then, accompanied by the security guard who'd met them upon their arrival. The two men stomped snow off their boots onto a straw mat. Virgil was trying to rub some circulation back into his ears. The camera hung from a strap around his neck.

"Joy's the only one who saw him leave then?"

Joy Yeaky lifted her head. Her green eyes were now red rimmed. "Nobody else was around when Mr.

Thornton left. I was reading, so I might not have noticed, either, if he hadn't stopped at the desk to tell me where he'd be.''

Something about the evasive shift of her gaze made Mitch wonder if she was telling the entire truth about what transpired when Thornton left the lodge. But if she was holding something back, it didn't necessarily follow that it concerned Thornton's death. There was little point in pressing her now in any case. The autopsy findings might make further interrogation unnecessary. He fervently hoped so.

''Have Mr. Thornton's mother and wife been notified?'' Mitch asked.

The three on the sofa looked at each other sheepishly. ''We decided to wait for you,'' Lucille said finally. ''I guess none of us wanted to be the one to tell them, especially Mr. Thornton's mother. She's depended on him so much since her husband died and she's been sick.''

''His wife hasn't called here, looking for him?'' Mitch asked. It was after eleven now. Surely Thornton was in the habit of getting home before this.

''They're separated,'' Lucille said. ''Mr. Thornton's been living here, in a suite. His wife stayed in their house.''

''In the same residential addition where LaDonna Thornton lives?'' Mitch asked.

''Yes, in Lakeview.''

Mitch hadn't known the Thorntons were separated, but they, like most of those living in the lake community, were newcomers, not really a part of the town. A few Buckskin families had built summer homes on the lake, but they lived in town nine or ten months out of the year.

Mitch got up and joined Virgil and the security guard near the registration desk. "Mitch, this is Doyle Swimmer," Virgil said. "Mr. Swimmer, Chief of Police Mitchell Bushyhead."

The two men shook hands. "When did you come on duty, Mr. Swimmer?" Mitch asked.

Swimmer screwed up his eyes in cogitation. "Well, now, it was about ten forty-five, I reckon. I was nearly an hour late, you see, 'cause my car got stuck in a drift. Covered up plumb past the front doors. Had to crawl out the back. Then I walked a ways to find a phone. Good thing I had on two pairs of long johns under my clothes. Waited till the wrecker came, and they hauled me and my car on out of here. We saw Lucille's pickup in the ditch just off the road. She was gonna call them in the morning, but since they were here she had 'em go ahead and do it. Lucille told me about Mr. Thornton. I went out and looked at him, but he was past helping—stone-cold dead."

The talkative Swimmer had been there barely thirty minutes then.

"Who did you relieve?"

"Brian Merchant. Young fella just graduated high school last year. He was going to the kitchen when Joy found Mr. Thornton. He's the one said they should leave the Bronco door open and everything else the way they found it. Brian's got his head screwed on straight."

"Where was he when Mr. Thornton left the lodge at seven forty-five?"

"In the security booth out front. We got a heater in there."

"So he didn't see Mr. Thornton leaving?"

"Nope. He stayed in the booth till right before Joy found Mr. Thornton. Brian thought I might not make it to work at all, so he was coming in to make a fresh pot of coffee for his thermos when he heard the ruckus."

Mitch thanked him and went back to the three on the sofa. "I don't have any more questions for you tonight," he said. "I may have to clarify a few things with you later. If you want to wait a while longer, Joy, Virgil can drive your Bronco back to town for you. Doc and I will follow and pick him up at your house, after we've notified Mr. Thornton's wife and mother."

The young woman nodded gratefully. "Thanks. I'm still pretty shaky. I'll call my husband and tell him I'll be later than I thought."

"Right now, I'd like to see Mr. Thornton's suite," Mitch said.

"I'll get a key," Lucille offered. "We keep a master at the registration desk."

She brought the key and Mitch asked, "Has anybody been in there since Mr. Thornton left?"

"Not that I know of," Lucille said. Billy and Joy shook their heads in agreement. "The suite's down that hall at the end. One fifteen."

Mitch motioned for Sullivan and Virgil to accompany him.

The suite consisted of three large rooms furnished in contemporary style, the furniture clean of line, a lot of leather and brass. A sitting room with a bath and two bedrooms opening off it on either side. There were no cooking facilities. Thornton would have taken his meals in the lodge dining room.

The three men glanced into both bedrooms. The beds were made and all the rooms were neat and clean.

Sullivan moved into the room with the king-size bed while Mitch and Virgil checked out the bathroom.

A white marble whirlpool tub filled half the room. The vanity was a deep, black marble bowl on a pedestal. Black and white towels hung on brass racks. Virgil bent over the vanity to lift something from the bowl with thumb and forefinger. "Look here, Mitch." A long blond hair dangled from Virgil's fingers. "Maybe we should save it."

"Might as well."

Virgil took a plastic sandwich bag from his uniform pocket, dropping the hair into it. He sealed the bag and used a ballpoint pen to write identifying information on a label, which he then peeled off its backing and stuck to the bag.

Mitch moved to the wastebasket beside the lavatory and looked through its contents. There was a lipstick-smeared tissue, which he handed to Virgil without a word. Virgil bagged and labeled the tissue.

"You suppose this suite is cleaned every day, same as the guest rooms?"

"Sure looks like it," Virgil said.

"If so, Thornton had a lady visitor sometime today, a blonde."

"There's a blonde sitting out in the lobby now."

"Let's not jump to conclusions. Could be a dozen blondes working here, not to mention guests. Could even have been somebody from outside."

"What about his wife?"

"She has red hair," Mitch said.

"Mitch, you want to come here a minute?" Sullivan called.

Mitch and Virgil found the doctor still in the bedroom with the king-size bed. The room had a door leading to the outside, Mitch noticed now.

Sullivan held an insulin bottle in each hand, one full, the other about two-thirds full. He held up the full bottle. "I got this one out of the refrigerator." He gestured toward a small refrigerator built into a storage unit. He held up the other bottle. "This one was on the bedside table." He turned both bottles so Mitch and Virgil could see the labels. "See, same lot number."

Mitch nodded, wondering what Sullivan was getting at. The doctor handed the partially used bottle to Mitch and rolled the other one between his hands. "Do this," he instructed, and Mitch followed Sullivan's example. Both bottles became cloudy as the motion mixed the white sediment at the bottom with the clear liquid.

"Notice anything?" Sullivan asked.

"Your bottle looks cloudier than mine."

"Exactly." Sullivan walked to the bedside table and picked up yet another partially full vial. It had no sediment in the bottom but was perfectly clear. "This is regular human insulin," Sullivan said, "U 100. That is, a hundred units of insulin per milliliter. These other two are NPH, a longer-acting insulin than U 100."

Seeing Mitch's frown, Sullivan added, "NPH works sort of like a twelve-hour cold capsule. It doesn't kick in as soon as regular insulin, and its effects last longer. Regular insulin starts to act thirty minutes to an hour after injection, and its action peaks in three to five hours. NPH doesn't kick in until about an hour and a half after injection, and it peaks seven to fifteen hours later."

"What's your point, Doc?" Mitch asked.

"Bear with me a minute, okay? Most diabetics take a combination of regular insulin and NPH. Because of NPH's longer action, some diabetics require only one injection a day. But Graham Thornton was on two a day, one a half hour before breakfast, the other a half hour before dinner. His evening dosage was twenty units of NPH and ten units of U 100, which he probably took sometime before he left the lodge."

"But why is your bottle of NPH cloudier than Mitch's?" Virgil asked.

"Good question," Sullivan said. "I think you ought to have these two vials of NPH analyzed. Might as well take that U 100 he was using, too."

"What do you expect to find, Doc?" Mitch asked.

"I'm not sure, but all vials of NPH, especially from the same lot, should look the same when you shake them up."

Mitch lifted his partially used vial of NPH. "You saying somebody tampered with one of these?"

"Let's just check it out," Sullivan said. "What's wrong?"

"We've ruined any fingerprints that were on these bottles."

"I didn't think about that," Sullivan said. "Sorry."

Mitch dropped all three vials into his jacket pocket. "I hear the ambulance," Virgil said. After another quick look around, the three men exited the suite.

A few minutes later, the ambulance left, carrying Thornton's body to the hospital in Buckskin, where it would remain until the medical examiner arrived from Tahlequah. Mitch left Virgil at the lodge, taking Sullivan with him to call on the two Mrs. Thorntons, since the doctor had seen them as patients. Lucille Hummingbird had given them directions to both addresses.

Magda Thornton's sprawling stone house was dark. Mitch rang the bell several times before she came to the door, a flannel robe thrown on over her gown, her dark red hair tousled.

The porch light flicked on and the door opened a crack. "Yes?"

"Sorry to disturb you, Mrs. Thornton. I'm Mitchell Bushyhead, with the Buckskin Police Department. I have Dr. Sullivan with me."

She opened the door wider, squinting at them. "What is it?"

"May we come in?"

"Oh. I'm sorry. Yes, please."

The living room was white—walls, carpet, sofa, and love seat. The low tables were made of glass and chrome. The only color was in the pictures on the walls and two mauve wingback chairs facing each other in front of the white stone fireplace.

"What's happened?" Magda Thornton asked from the living room doorway. She hadn't followed them into the room but was stationed in the foyer, as though she wanted to go back to bed and didn't want to make them feel too comfortable, lest they linger.

She was a handsome woman. Some might say beautiful. Good bones and porcelain skin. She had a way of carrying herself that Mitch could only describe as regal. She was of medium height, but her carriage made her appear taller.

"Magda," Sullivan said gently, "come here and sit down. We have bad news, I'm afraid."

She came into the room then and allowed Sullivan to take her hand and lead her to the sofa. She looked up at them with calm brown eyes.

Sullivan sat down beside her. "We're here about Graham, Magda. He died this evening."

"Graham? Dead?" She looked puzzled. Then came a faint flicker of the brown eyes and a barely perceptible sagging of the proud shoulders. She might have just learned her cat, whom she didn't care all that much for to begin with, had been run over. "Who killed him?"

"What makes you think he was killed?" Mitch asked.

She looked at him steadily, then shook her head. She allowed herself a long breath. Leaned back. "It was the first thing that came to mind. I don't know why, except that Graham alienates—alienated people."

"How?"

She combed red-tipped fingers through gleaming copper-colored hair, which fell in expertly cut layers. "By being his usual obnoxious self."

Sullivan shifted uncomfortably on the sofa. "We don't know how he died yet. He was found in an employee's car at the lodge. It might have been cardiac arrest. We can't tell without an autopsy."

"I guess you need my permission for that," she said calmly, "since technically we're still married."

"No ma'am," Mitch said. "An autopsy is required by law when cause of death can't be determined without it."

"I see. Well, thank you for—" She halted and sat forward. "Does LaDonna know yet?"

"We're going there from here," Mitch said.

"This will kill her." Her voice changed, became efficient, more animated. She rose. "Give me a minute to change, and I'll come with you. Cara's probably out gallivanting. That's all she's done since she came home for Christmas break. She wouldn't be much help anyway, and LaDonna will need somebody with her tonight." She strode purposefully from the room.

"A proud woman," Sullivan muttered. "Tremendous control."

She had been so unrelentingly cool until they mentioned her mother-in-law. Maybe it was one of those cases where in-laws remained good friends after a marriage ended.

"That's not control," Mitch said. "It's indifference."

As it turned out, Mitch was glad Magda came along. LaDonna Thornton began crying before they finished telling her why they were there. As soon as Sullivan mentioned Graham, she seemed to know it was bad news. Why else would the three of them have come to her house on such a night?

They'd awakened her, and she stood in her den in a cream-colored satin robe, amidst a lot of dark, ornate furniture, refusing to sit down until Sullivan stopped talking. At which point her silent tears turned to racking sobs.

Magda put her arms around her, patted her back, and said, "I know, LaDonna, I know."

LaDonna Thornton looked very pale to Mitch, and he remembered that, on top of the shock, she'd been sick. Her long silver hair was braided in a single plait for the night, and somehow that made her look defenseless. She winced when Magda touched her and pushed her arms away as though she couldn't stand to be handled by the friend who'd been in the process of divorcing her son, now that he was dead. She hugged herself and struggled to stop weeping.

"You'd better sit down, LaDonna," Sullivan said.

She regained some measure of composure and murmured. "Yes, yes, I'd better. I've not been well." She crept unsteadily to the couch, half bent over, touching chairs and lamps en route like a blind person.

Sullivan opened his medical bag and shook several capsules into the palm of his hand. "I'll leave some tranquilizers," he said to Magda. "See that she takes one every six hours for a couple of days." To La-Donna, he said, "You should have come to see me when you first felt ill. Have you had any fever?"

LaDonna sat erect on the edge of the couch and placed her blue-veined hands on her knees, as though to brace herself. "None in the last forty-eight hours. It's the old-fashioned flu. I've been getting plenty of rest and liquids."

"You act as though your ribs are sore."

"Just a little."

"You could have a touch of pneumonia. I'd better listen to your chest."

She waved Sullivan's stethoscope away. "Never mind me. The soreness is almost gone." She took a tissue from the pocket of her robe and wiped her eyes. "Tell me what happened. Where is Graham?"

"At the hospital," Sullivan said. "He can be moved to the funeral home later, probably tomorrow, after the autopsy."

She winced at the mention of an autopsy.

"We don't know yet how he died," Mitch added. "According to an employee at the lodge, he left there at seven forty-five. It appears he never got any farther than the parking lot. Joy Yeaky found him in her Bronco when she went out to go home at ten."

LaDonna blinked in confusion. "In Joy's...? I don't understand."

"Neither do we," Mitch said. "When he left the lodge, he told Joy he was coming here. Were you expecting him?"

"No, but he often drops in unexpectedly"—she glanced at Magda and then away—"since he moved out of his house."

Mitch saw Magda press her lips together, probably to keep from reminding her mother-in-law that the house was as much hers as Graham's. Mitch wondered if the terms of the divorce settlement had been agreed upon. Magda had probably expected to get decent alimony payments and perhaps full title to the house. Now, he supposed, since she was still Graham's wife, she'd inherit everything. From what he'd heard, everything could run into seven figures.

"You didn't see him at all this evening?"

"No."

"Where's Cara?" Magda asked suddenly.

LaDonna still seemed stunned by the news of her son's death. She hesitated, as if trying to remember where her daughter might have gone, before she said, "Out with Michael—her fiancé," the "fiancé" added for Mitch's and Sullivan's benefit. "They left here at eight, in the middle of the storm if you can believe it. I tried to talk them out of making that drive, but no..." She pressed a hand to her mouth for an instant. "Cara called from Tulsa about ten and said they wouldn't be back tonight. I suppose they'll be here tomorrow if they can get through." Her pale hands twisted the belt of her robe. "Oh, dear, she doesn't know about Graham, and I didn't even ask where they were staying tonight. She didn't give me a chance."

"Tomorrow will be soon enough," Magda said. "I'll stay with you tonight, if you like."

"Yes, please, Magda," she said distractedly. "So thoughtful of you."

"We'll get out of your way then," Mitchell said.

The two men drove back to the lodge. "Magda Thornton sure wasn't cut up over the news," Mitch observed. "She seemed almost relieved."

"There were hard feelings," Sullivan said. "I hear the divorce negotiations have been nasty."

After picking up Virgil at the Yeaky house, Mitch and Virgil drove Sullivan home and headed toward the police station. They met no other cars. Sequoyah, the main street, was smothered in snow that had blown high drifts against the buildings on the east side of the street. The scrunch of the Land Cruiser's tires sounded unnaturally loud in the white silence. It felt as though the whole town were holding its breath.

"Billy Choate thinks Thornton was killed by a night walker," Virgil said.

Mitch darted a look at him. "A Cherokee witch?" He understood why Choate had waited until he and Sullivan left before telling Virgil. Although Mitch was half Cherokee, he hadn't grown up among his father's people. He would probably always be an outsider to certain elements of the tribe.

Virgil, on the other hand, had been born and raised in Buckskin. He was a member of the Nighthawk Keetowahs, a secret society of conservative Cherokees dedicated to preserving the old ways. Even if Virgil didn't accept the existence of night walkers, which Mitch wouldn't have bet on either way, he'd understand and respect those who did. Mitch had once commented on the seeming paradox that Virgil was a Nighthawk while remaining a faithful member of the

Baptist church. Virgil had said it was like having two insurance policies.

"Billy told me he's heard a screech owl near the lodge for three nights running," Virgil said.

"That means it's a night walker?"

"Billy's convinced of it."

"I wondered why he was so nervous."

"He's so scared he won't leave the lodge tonight. Says he might quit his job, though he doesn't know where he'll get another one."

"Joy Yeaky was mighty shook up, too."

"Maybe she never saw a dead person before, not for real—somebody she knew."

"I wonder just how well she did know Thornton. She called him Graham, then corrected herself. Did you notice?"

"Yeah, but didn't you tell me not to jump to conclusions? She's married, isn't she?"

"That doesn't always stop people."

"No kidding."

Mitch grunted. "If this turns out to be suspicious, we'll have to pry out people's secrets. Everybody has 'em, just like everybody's got problems."

Virgil glanced at him. "Why do I get the feeling you're talking about yourself now?"

Mitch's mouth twisted wryly. "Emily found out about Lisa."

"Before you told her, like I been after you to do?"

"I was waiting for the right time." Mitch laughed shortly. "Tonight sure as hell wasn't it."

"She probably feels threatened. Doesn't want to share you. She'll come around."

"You think so?"

"Emily's basically a sensible kid. Anyway, what choice does she have?"

"I hope she comes to that conclusion soon. I'm getting tired of sitting around that house talking to myself."

"I told you to tell her."

"You already said that."

SIX

Friday, December 15

MITCH BURROWED into his pillow, clinging to the remnants of sleep. Water. Dripping. It was raining. He rolled over and eased one eye open a slit. The sunlight flooding through his bedroom window nearly blinded him. His eye snapped shut. It wasn't rain; it was a small river of melted snow pouring off the steep-pitched roof.

Yesterday the temperature had climbed twenty degrees in three hours, and from what Mitch had seen in that one brief peek, today would hold more of the same. The eleven inches of snow that had fallen four days ago, and virtually paralyzed Buckskin until Tuesday afternoon when the streets department got around to sanding the main thoroughfares, would be little more than patches of slush and a memory by the weekend. Unless another storm dumped more snow on Buckskin within the next ten days, there would be no white Christmas.

He squinted at the red numerals on his clock radio. Eight ten. He should have been up an hour ago.

He threw back the blanket and staggered to the bathroom. A shave and a hot shower made him feel almost human again. He dressed in a clean khaki uniform and was whistling softly as he left the bedroom.

Emily's door stood ajar. The lavender-and-pink ruffled curtains were tied back from the windows, and sunlight made a golden pathway across the oak floor. The bed was unmade, but Emily wasn't there.

Downstairs, a note was propped against the salt-shaker on the kitchen table: *Had to leave early for a meeting at school. Emily.*

No "Dear Daddy" or "Love." Nothing but the bare facts, ma'am. Emily was as grudging in her communication via the written word as the spoken. Since their confrontation over Lisa Macpherson last Monday night, Mitch had tried several times to discuss the situation with Emily. What had transpired was more of a monologue than a discussion. He could only hope she'd listened and would realize that she was being unreasonable, once she'd cooled off and thought it over.

Mitch didn't even take time to make coffee before he left the house. En route to the police station, he stopped at the doughnut shop on Highway 10 for a sugary cinnamon roll still warm from the oven and coffee in a Styrofoam cup.

He was still sipping the coffee when he walked into the station at eight forty. Helen Hendricks, the dispatcher, glanced up from a crossword puzzle. She was a tall woman with wide eyes that forever seemed to be assessing her workaday world with the long-suffering tolerance of a mother of four preschoolers, which she wasn't. Married to her third husband, Helen had no children.

"Busy morning, Helen?"

"Not so's you could tell it. You got a couple phone calls. I put the messages on your desk." Her newspaper rustled as she went back to the crossword puzzle.

Mitch drained the Styrofoam cup and refilled it from the pot in the common room. Harold "Duck" Duckworth and Charles "Roo" Stephens, the two officers who worked the day shift, were lounging in the far corner of the big room. Duck leaned back in his chair, his feet resting on the duty desk. Long-legged Roo sat on a corner of the desk, nursing a cup of coffee.

Duck made a production of pushing up his shirt-sleeve to peer at his watch. He gazed at Mitch ruefully with his close-set, mismatched eyes, one brown, the other hazel. "Carousing till all hours again, Chief? Better watch it. You ain't as young as you used to be."

Leave it to Duck to seize every opportunity to re-mind Mitch that his fortieth birthday was a scant three months away. "Few of us are what we used to be," Mitch said, staring pointedly at Duck's khaki shirt. It was stretched taut across his gut, the buttons ready to pop off. "Speaking of which, have you weighed in yet this week?"

Recently Mitch had instituted weight and fitness re-quirements for his officers. Feeling he should set the example, he'd bought an exercise bike for his office and put in forty-five minutes on it three or four times a week. Roo and Virgil planned to take up jogging as soon as the worst of the winter was past.

But Duck was the only member of the four-man force with a real weight problem. Mitch had suggested he use the exercise bike, too, but Duck hadn't. Mitch had seen him walking with his wife, Geraldine, a few times, around the high school track, and Duck claimed to be on a diet, but so far there was no noticeable weight loss.

Duck's feet slid off the desk and he sat up straight, trying to suck in his belly. "Lost another pound. That makes a total of four big ones."

"You've been on that diet eight weeks now," Mitch said.

"I got a sluggish thyroid."

A grin cracked Roo's freckled face. "It's not your thyroid. It's those four doughnuts you wolf down every morning, like they were going out of style."

Duck's round face reddened. "I haven't eaten four doughnuts at once since I started this diet."

"Okay, you spread 'em out over the morning. Pardon me."

"You got no idea what it's like, having a metabolism that just sits there, not doing anything."

Roo rolled his eyes toward the ceiling. "Next you'll tell us you've got big bones."

Duck hunched forward and scowled at a glass paperweight on the desk. "Easy for you to talk. You're a walking skeleton. Wouldn't surprise me if you got a tapeworm."

"You need to quit making excuses."

"I'm not," Duck said sulkily. "I been trying, I tell you."

"Yeah, you try for a day, maybe two. Then you go on a binge and undo all the good you've done."

"Maybe I have slipped off my diet once or twice. So shoot me."

Roo hooted. "Once or twice! More like once or twice a day. You have any idea how many calories are in one doughnut? Or that blackberry cobbler with ice cream you ate at the Three Squares yesterday?"

Roo wasn't usually so relentless, and Mitch was rather enjoying the exchange. Duck had razzed Roo unmercifully for months, ever since Roo had started dating Laura Tucker, a young woman who worked at the local library and Roo's first serious girlfriend. It amused Mitch to see Duck get his comeuppance for a change.

Duck was not amused, though. "What is this, Roo? You spying on me now, keeping track of everything I eat?"

"Nobody has to keep track. Flab speaks for itself. Geez, you're your own worst enemy, Duck." Roo sounded very earnest now. In spite of often being the brunt of Duck's crude jokes, he liked the man. "You're gonna get put on probation if you don't lose some of that fat." Finally, he shrugged and turned away. "Oh, well. I'm going over to the Kirkwood sisters' house."

"Somebody trying to ravish them again?" Mitch asked. Polly and Millicent Kirkwood were spinster sisters in their seventies who shared a paranoid conviction that dangerous men tailed them wherever they went, leaving an accomplice behind to rifle their house. According to Polly and Millicent, they had barely escaped being raped times too numerous to mention, the randy housebreaker having left by the back way as the sisters walked in the front.

"Miss Polly says somebody moved her knitting from the table where she left it when she went out to get the morning newspaper. Says it couldn't have been Millicent because she was still asleep. She wants me to put another lock on her back door for her."

"They ever heard of a locksmith?" Duck grumbled.

"That'd deprive them of the excitement of having a police car parked at their house for all the neighbors to see," Mitch said.

"What those two old gals need is a good lay. That'd open up a whole new world for 'em. Give 'em something to think about besides their fantasies."

A weary sigh was heard from Helen's end of the room.

"You volunteering for the job?" Roo asked.

Duck snorted. "That's more your department, Roo. You're the big stud, judging from Laura Tucker's contented expression these days."

Roo's Adam's apple bobbed. He gave Duck a disdainful look, then departed with his awkward, loping kangaroo gait. Roo's high school basketball teammates had nicknamed him Kangaroo, quickly shortening it to Roo, and it had stuck.

Mitch lingered at the duty desk. "You agreed to lose twenty pounds by the end of January," he reminded Duck, "and another twenty by June."

"You're as bad as Geraldine, like a broken record," Duck whined. "Cut me some slack, Chief. I'm starving as it is."

"We'll feed you intravenously if you faint," Helen called over her shoulder, "and then get you laid, since you think that'll solve anything."

Shaking his head, Mitch went to his office. He hung his jacket on the coatrack and picked up the pink phone-message slips. Bob Devay, the mayor, had returned Mitch's call of the day before. Mitch wanted to make sure the subject of an additional police officer was on the agenda for the next City Council meeting. He'd get back to Devay later in the day.

He tossed that slip into the wastebasket and scanned the second message. Ken Pohl, the medical examiner, had phoned and requested that Mitch call him back as soon as possible.

Mitch reached for the receiver and dialed the Tahlequah number. A secretary put him straight through to Pohl. "Sorry I couldn't get back to you sooner on the Thornton case, Mitch. I'm up to my eyeballs in paper here. Federal forms. State forms. To think I went to medical school because I wanted to practice forensic medicine—maybe teach a class on the side. They don't mention you have to be a damn clerk, too. It's a conspiracy, I tell you."

"It's rough all over, Doc."

"It certainly was rough for Graham Thornton."

"Could you skip the medical jargon and give it to me in layman's language?"

"Sure. To simplify, Thornton went into insulin shock, lost consciousness, unfortunately in a subfreezing temperature, and wasn't found for two or three hours. When the body temperature drops low enough, the heart stops. He might have died anyway, but exposure to the cold undoubtedly hastened it."

"Are you saying there's no evidence of foul play?" Mitch asked hopefully.

"I'm getting to that. I have the lab analysis of the contents of those vials. The full vial of NPH and the partially full U 100 check out fine. The other NPH, the one Thornton was using, is adulterated."

"Adulterated?"

"About two thirds of the NPH insulin has been removed and replaced with U 100."

"That's why it wasn't as cloudy as the full bottle."

"Correct."

"Doc Sullivan said Thornton gave himself an injection of twenty units of NPH and ten units of U 100 sometime before he left the lodge that night. You're saying somebody changed those proportions. He got more U 100 and less NPH. Am I right?"

"On the nose, Mitch. You can't pin it down that tight with an autopsy, but the insulin is very strong circumstantial evidence that that's what happened."

"Could that throw him into insulin shock?"

"You bet. You see, he got a rush of insulin all at once, somewhere between a half hour to an hour after injection, because there was too much U 100 in the doctored dosage."

"So...it hit him about the time he reached the parking lot. But wouldn't he have had some warning?"

"A feeling of euphoria accompanies the onset of insulin shock. The victim may not realize he's in trouble until it's too late. By the time Thornton realized it—if he ever did—he was probably extremely disoriented. Diabetics in that condition have been jailed for drunkenness. Thornton may have thought he was getting into his own car when he crawled into that Bronco. Or maybe it was the closest vehicle and he knew he couldn't make it any farther, but he still had enough presence of mind to seek shelter from the storm."

"If he'd yelled or honked the horn—"

"He wasn't thinking that clearly. I'd guess he barely managed to get out of the weather before he passed out."

And left the Bronco door open so the blizzard could blow in on him. Mitch sighed.

"It's not a painful way to die, Mitch."

"But he's just as dead. I've got a murder on my hands, not to mention a fifteen-year-old daughter who disapproves of me."

"All fifteen-year-old kids disapprove of their parents, Mitch. It's required."

Mitch grunted.

"Has she developed the 'Are you sure I'm not adopted?' syndrome yet?"

"No."

"Well, there you are. Something to look forward to."

"By golly, Doc, I'm glad we had this little talk. You sure know how to cheer a guy up."

"Glad to do my bit for the upholders of law and order, Mitch. Any time. It's rough all over."

"Yeah, yeah."

"I'll mail you a copy of the autopsy report and the lab analysis on the insulin today."

"Obliged, Doc."

Mitch's swivel chair squeaked as he turned to stare out his office window at Buckskin's sun-drenched main street, Sequoyah. Except for the remains of the snowstorm, it looked more like September than December. Which could change quickly. Okalahoma's weather could go from one extreme to the other with little warning.

Melted snow ran down the gutters on either side of Sequoyah and gushed into storm drains. People who'd been shut in their houses and businesses the past few days were scurrying to the post office and the drugstore, sloshing through the dirty slush on the sidewalk. Directly across the street, in the building that had once housed a shoe store, the new needlework shop opened by two local women seemed to be doing a brisk business this morning. The Christmas decorations hanging over the street—plastic Santas and reindeer—shone brightly in the sunlight.

He turned back to his desk, to the accompaniment of the squeaking chair. He took the snapshots of Graham Thornton's body from a drawer and spread them out on his desk. Thornton's twisted mouth gaped at him from all of them. According to Pohl, it hadn't been a painful death. Yet Thornton looked horrified.

Had he known in his last moment of consciousness that he was dying?

Mitch slid the pictures back into a drawer and reached for his jacket, shrugging into it as he left the office. "Duck, let's get it in gear," he called. "We have business out at Eagle's Nest Lodge."

"Try not to miss me too much, Helen," Duck said as they passed the dispatcher's desk.

"God, it'll be hard. But I'll be strong."

On the drive to the lodge, Mitch filled Duck in on what he'd learned from the medical examiner. "Good thing Doc Sullivan went into Thornton's suite with us Monday night. Virgil and I might not have noticed there was something wrong with that insulin."

"You think Thornton would have noticed, when he started to inject himself."

"Not really. You do the same thing every day for years, it's an ingrained habit."

"You see what you expect to see."

"Yeah. He probably glanced at the labels, then drew the insulin into the syringe, paying no attention to how it looked. He'd been doing it for nearly twenty years. He could probably do it with his eyes closed."

"Thornton's funeral service is this afternoon," Duck said. "I saw the announcement in the paper."

"We'll tackle the employees first and get to the family members next week."

"The perp's the wife," Duck said confidently. Mitch winced at his use of the TV slang. Duck had been watching cop shows again. "They were getting a divorce."

"I heard."

"The Thorntons hated each other. He was trying to cut her off without a cent. Claimed she didn't have anything coming because she was the one wanted the divorce, not him. She was fighting for half of everything."

"You heard all this from Geraldine?" Duck's wife worked as a waitress at the Three Squares Cafe on Highway 10. The waitresses heard every scrap of gossip that hit Buckskin within hours of its arrival and felt it their civic duty to spread it further.

Duck nodded. "She overheard Magda Thornton talking to her lawyer about it."

"Who's the lawyer?"

"Jack Derring."

"Wonderful." Mitch hadn't known Derring took divorce cases. Young Jack Derring had made a name for himself as an ambitious criminal lawyer. Last September, Derring had been counsel for the defense in a murder trial. Mitch had been one of three witnesses to the shooting. The extenuating circumstances didn't alter the fact that it looked like premeditated murder. Undaunted, Derring had claimed the shooting was accidental. He'd presented a dramatic, emotional-charged defense that had the jurors eating out of his hand.

When the dust settled, Derring's client received a six-year sentence and would probably be out on probation in eighteen months.

Mitch disliked Derring, having opposed the cocky son of a gun too often in a courtroom. Now he'd probably have to question him about the Thorntons' divorce negotiations. Not that it would get him anywhere. Derring wouldn't give him the time of day if he was sitting in a room full of grandfather clocks. With any luck, Magda Thornton would open up about it, and he wouldn't have to go to Derring.

"Seems like we can't do business without tangling with Derring on a regular basis," Duck observed.

Mitch turned off the highway on the quarter-mile black-topped lane leading to the lodge. "No job is perfect. Life is full of little inconveniences." He waved at the young security officer who thrust his head out of the guard booth. Mitch parked in the circular drive near the glass-paneled entry.

"Tell me about it," Duck puffed as he climbed out of the patrol car. "Take me. Why couldn't I have been born rich instead of so goll-derned good-looking?"

The two women at the registration desk watched a bit apprehensively as Mitch and Duck approached. The mere sight of a police uniform made some people think of the pencil they stole in third grade or the candy bar they snitched when they were twelve. The women were both in their forties, one on the plump side, the other downright obese.

After introducing himself and Duck, Mitch learned the women's names, Judy Browne and Pansy Nibell. He questioned them about Graham Thornton's comings and goings the day he died. Neither woman had noticed anything unusual in Thornton's behavior or activities that day, but they had left at two. Nor could they say who had entered Thornton's suite, except for one of the maids, of course. Mitch would have to talk to them to find out which one had cleaned the suite last Monday.

As an afterthought, Mitch said, "I don't suppose any of the Thorntons is around this morning."

"Mr. Thornton's sister is in his office," Pansy Nibell, the fat woman, said, her chins jiggling. "It's down that hall, first door on the right."

An unexpected piece of luck. Mitch hadn't met the younger sister, Cara, whom Magda Thornton had described as "gallivanting" and not much use in a crisis. He was eager to do so. He motioned for Duck to follow him.

The secretary was not at her desk. Probably had the day off to attend the funeral. The sounds of desk drawers banging open and closed came from the inner office. The door stood ajar.

The desk was covered with folders, stacks of loose papers, ledgerlike notebooks, two framed photographs lying glass down, three coffee cups, and numerous expensive-looking ballpoint pens, obviously the contents of the desk drawers that Cara Thornton was emptying. Cara was doubled over behind the desk, rifling through the bottom drawer and muttering to herself.

"Miss Thornton?"

Short, springy black curls appeared above the desktop, followed by big blue eyes set in an oval face with a dark smudge across the short nose and one pink cheek. She stared at them in astonishment as she straightened and rose from a tan leather chair. She was dressed in a tight yellow sweater and jeans that left none of her body's fetching curves to the imagination.

"Officer?" The clipped voice rose in inquiry.

"I'm Chief Mitchell Bushyhead of the Buckskin Police, Miss Thornton, and this is Officer Duckworth. We'd like to ask you a few questions, if you're feeling up to it."

She came around the desk and leaned back against it, bracing herself with her hands behind her. The pose, which Mitch suspected was calculated, clearly exposed the outlines of her nipples beneath the yellow sweater. She wore no bra.

In Duck's opinion, she could have posed for the centerfold in one of the girlie magazines he leafed through at the drugstore, when no one was watching. She flicked a cursory glance in his direction. He sucked in his stomach and, with a businesslike flourish, reached into his shirt pocket for his pen and small spiral notebook.

"I feel fine, but I'm extremely busy, as you can see. Somebody has to clear out Graham's junk. I didn't want Mother to have to deal with it."

"Will you be helping your mother with the lodge now?"

"Me?" She looked as shocked as though Mitch had suggested she take up digging ditches. "No way! I'm planning an extended trip through Europe after the holidays." She delivered this announcement with such a determined thrust of her chin that Mitch wondered who she expected to contradict her. Her gaze followed Duck as he waddled to a chair and settled on its arm. When he looked at her, a flush crept up his neck. She returned her gaze to Mitch. "Why are you here? I didn't know the police took an interest in natural deaths."

"There's been a new development. Somebody tampered with your brother's insulin."

Cara gave an irritated little snort, walked around behind the desk and stood with her back to them, staring out the window. "That's ridiculous. He had a heart attack, like my father."

"Not according to the medical examiner. I'll be glad to send you and your mother copies of the autopsy report and the lab analysis of the insulin we took from his room.''

She stepped to the walnut credenza against the wall and jerked the stopper from a cut-glass decanter. She sloshed brandy into a tumbler. The hand that lifted the tumbler to her mouth shook a little. She swallowed, grimaced as though it were medicine, then grasped the tumbler with both hands. Brilliant blue eyes focused on Mitch abruptly. ''What has this to do with me?''

''Who had reason to want your brother dead?''

She took another gulp of brandy and set the tumbler down on a bare corner of the desk. She laughed and the sound had a shrill edge to it. ''Who wanted him dead? How much time do you have? The people who didn't want him dead would make a shorter list.''

Mitch remembered Magda Thornton's words: *Graham alienated people.* ''Murder is an extreme and desperate act, Miss Thornton. It's hard to believe he could have done something bad enough to warrant it.''

She dropped into the chair behind the desk, gripped the arms—to keep her hands steady? Mitch wondered—and gave the two officers a couldn't-care-less smile. Duck eyed the ripe curves pressing against the yellow sweater and the tumbled black curls, and his fair skin flushed a brighter pink than before. Mitch frowned at him, and he ducked his head and began making studious notes.

''You wouldn't say that if you'd known him,'' she said. ''My brother manipulated, intimidated, connived, lied—whatever it took to get what he wanted. People were objects to him, to be moved around to suit his purposes.'' She tossed her ebony curls back and stared at Mitch boldly. A tiny vein throbbed beneath the creamy skin of her throat, betraying an otherwise nonchalant facade.

Briefly Mitch felt sorry for her. She was only a few years older than Emily, so young to be carrying around such a load of anger and resentment. "You hated your brother, didn't you?"

She frowned at Mitch in a rather impersonal way, as if wondering why he kept bothering her with those tiresome questions. "Let's just say we didn't get along."

Mitch couldn't think of the venom with which she had spoken of her brother as the outcome of merely "not getting along." There was far more than sibling rivalry here. "Why? What did he do to you?"

"It wasn't *me* in particular." But Mitch thought it was. "Graham didn't play favorites. He made everybody miserable, simply on general principle. Ask his wife." A sadness flickered across her face. "My life hasn't been the same since my father died—but no more. Oh, no. So, don't expect me to cry crocodile tears because somebody killed Graham. The wonder is nobody did it before now." She picked up the tumbler and drank the last of the brandy, eyeing them defiantly over the rim. As she set the empty tumbler on the credenza, she said, "You can't arrest me for not being hypocrite enough to mourn my brother's death, can you?"

Mitch stared at her for a long moment. Was she actually as unfeeling as she appeared, or was she one of those young people who did and said appalling things merely for the shock value? He wasn't sure, so he asked, "Where were you Monday?"

At first, he thought she wasn't going to answer. She folded her arms and gazed at the jumbled items on the desk. Then slowly she looked up. "You mean Monday night? I went to Tulsa with my fiancé, Michael Harp. He's a med student at OU. He's staying at his parents' home in Muskogee over Christmas break." She smiled cunningly. "You can check my alibi with Michael or with my mother."

"And earlier in the day?"

She lifted a dark eyebrow. "What time?"

"From the time you got up in the morning."

She rolled her eyes, reminding him of Emily. "Do I look like the sort of girl who writes down every little thing in a diary? Really! This is all so unnecessary, anyway."

"On the contrary, Miss Thornton. Your brother's insulin could have been tampered with any time after his morning injection and before, say, seven thirty that evening. Were you in the lodge during those hours?"

She picked up a folder from the desk and started leafing through its contents, illustrating her lack of concern. "Actually," she murmured as though half her mind were elsewhere, "I tried never to go where I'd be likely to run into Graham, if I could help it." She closed the folder and tossed it onto the desk. "If you must have a blow-by-blow account, I slept late—until sometime after eleven, then had brunch with my mother. After that, the snow started; so I just slouched around the house until Michael came at about seven forty-five, and we left for Tulsa."

"We'll ask your mother to corroborate your testimony, of course."

She opened her eyes wide in a rather theatrical expression of startlement. "Testimony? I didn't know I was on the witness stand, Chief Bushyhead."

"A figure of speech," Mitch said, "but if you'd like to change anything you've told us..."

"Of course not."

"Officer Duckworth will type your statement. Someone will be back, after the weekend, to ask you to sign it. You'll be at your mother's house?"

"Yes."

"Well, thank you."

When they left the office, Mitch heard her punching out a number on the telephone.

In the lobby, Mitch spoke to Pansy Nibell at the registration desk. "I want to talk to all employees who were in the lodge Monday. Would—"

Pansy Nibell looked pained as a young boy streaked through the lobby to the door. "Jimmy!" she called. "Jimmy, did your mother give you permission to go out?"

The boy yelled, "Yes!" then stuck his tongue out, tugged open the door, and ran outside.

"Don't go far," Pansy said to the closed door. She looked around uncertainly. "Oh, dear. A real terror, that one. His parents came here to rest, and they seem to have given him the run of the place. He's only five, too. What will he be at sixteen?"

Mitch didn't care to predict. At five, Emily had been a charming, obedient little girl, but lately... "As I was saying, would it be possible for you to give me a list of employees who worked Monday?"

"Why—er, I suppose so." She patted her hair with chubby, beringed fingers. "The work schedule for the following week is distributed to employees every Friday. I can probably find my copy of this week's schedule." She pulled open a few drawers and finally located the schedule. When she straightened up, she was red-faced and breathless. She handed the schedule to Mitch.

"Thank you. Can one of you ladies bring the employees to me, as I call for them?"

"I can do that." Pansy patted her hair again, preening importantly. She seemed to be envisioning herself in the role of detective's sidekick. Young Jimmy was forgotten. "We're not busy today. You just tell me who you want to see first."

"Fine. I'll need a room for the interviews."

She looked less sure now. "Oh, you'd have to clear that with somebody in authority."

"Will you dial Mrs. Thornton for me?"

She didn't move. "I'd rather not do that. I had to call the house about something earlier, and Magda Thornton said Mrs. Thornton was sleeping and she didn't want to wake her unless it was an emergency."

"Then is there anyone else I can ask?"

She smiled almost apologetically. "If you wouldn't mind, you could talk to Miss Thornton." She glanced toward the hall leading to Graham Thornton's office. "I'm sure that would be all right."

Mitch went over to the sofa where Duck was sitting, copying his notes in a more legible hand. "I'm going back to ask Cara Thornton for the use of a room where we can interview the employees." Duck nodded without looking up.

Mitch was halfway down the hall leading to the office. He stopped and listened. Cara Thornton's voice was raised, the words harsh with outrage. Mitch edged silently closer to the open door, keeping far enough back to remain out of sight.

"I've been listening to your legal double-talk for ten minutes, Mr. Dunlap. Cut the crap, okay?"

There was only one lawyer in Buckskin named Dunlap—Dewey Dunlap, a small, solemn-demeanored man in his sixties who practiced law from a cramped, old-fashioned office at the corner of Sequoyah and Osage, the same office utilized by his father and grandfather before him.

"I know my father left the money in a trust fund, damn it! Why do you keep telling me things I already know?"

The leather chair creaked as she shifted restlessly.

"What I want to know is how I can get the money before I'm thirty. Since Graham's dead, and he was the trustee, there must be some provision for that in the law." She paused only long enough for Dunlap to slip in a few words edgewise. "I don't have to answer to you! I certainly don't need your permission to drop out of school for a few months and travel in Europe—or on the moon, for that matter!"

In the silence, there was the sound of a hand slapping something hard—possibly the arm of her chair—with some force.

"I don't care what Graham said about it, you mealy-mouthed old coot! Graham wouldn't even give me enough of my own money to keep up a decent wardrobe. Heaven forbid, I should take off and have a little fun with some of what Daddy left me. What?"

There as a little choking sound. "Magda! I can understand Mother being named trustee in Graham's place, but I'll be damned if I'll let Magda tell me what to do.... Well, why wasn't it changed? Magda and Graham were getting a divorce, for God's sake."

The leather chair creaked loudly, as though she'd leaped out of it. "Are you saying you won't discuss my trust fund with me until after the reading of the will next Monday? I don't believe this! Listen to me, Dunlap—'' She was yelling now. ''I can handle my mother.'' There was a touch of contempt in the words. ''As for Magda, she'd better stay out of my way. And *you* had better have a full accounting of my investments by Monday—to the penny. Do you hear me?'' The receiver banged into its cradle.

Mitch retreated back down the hall and waited a full minute before retracing his steps. In the interim, he heard Cara Thornton shoveling things from the top of Graham Thornton's desk into drawers, then slamming them violently. Evidently she'd been searching for something—a record of her trust fund investments?—not cleaning out the desk, as she'd said.

SEVEN

VELA WHITTLE, the third employee Mitch interviewed, was a thin, chain-smoking woman with a bitter mouth like a prune. She hesitated at the door, an ash-laden cigarette clamped between her protruding teeth, then walked into the office vacated by Cara Thornton, who'd gone home.

"Guess it's my turn," she said, looking around for an ashtray. Mitch slid the one on the desk toward her. She picked it up, knocked the ash into it, and sat down in the chair facing Mitch. Duck sat on the sofa behind her, his spiral notebook ready.

"Ask your questions then," she said, puffing on her cigarette. "I got ten more rooms to clean. One of the maids didn't show up today. Indian. We got an Indian waiter off, too. They're all scared of their shadows since Mr. Thornton died. Something about Cherokee witches."

"I understand you cleaned Graham Thornton's suite Monday. Is that right?"

"Been checking up on me, eh? Yeah, the maid you just interviewed told me somebody done Mr. Thornton in." She made a slashing motion across her throat. "Maybe there is a witch loose around here." She cackled.

"She mentioned in passing that you cleaned Graham Thornton's suite."

"Hazel would." She harrumphed. "Likes to see other people get their tit in a wringer. Oops, 'scuse me."

"Did you, in fact, clean Graham Thornton's suite Monday?"

"Monday and every other day, except for my days off. The head housekeeper assigns us certain rooms. We don't switch around."

"That would be Nila Ridge."

She nodded, squashing out her cigarette in the ashtray and setting it on the corner of the desk. "This was supposed to be Nila's last day. I guess she'll be staying on now."

"You mean she resigned but has now changed her mind?"

"Oh, no. Mr. Thornton fired her."

"When was this?"

She lifted her bony shoulders. "Hazel didn't tell you? Thornton gave Nila notice—oh, it'd be about two weeks ago now."

"Do you know why?"

"I heard Mr. Thornton caught Nila sleeping in the storeroom. She don't make a habit of it, but he fired her anyway, like that." She snapped her work-roughened fingers.

Mitch looked at her silently, and she went on. "Nila went to Mrs. Thornton."

"LaDonna Thornton?"

She nodded. "She promised to take Nila's side with Mr. Thornton, but she's been sick." She shrugged again. "With Mr. Thornton out of the picture, Nila won't have to worry about her job. She needs it, poor woman." She pulled a crumpled pack from her uniform pocket and tapped out a cigarette, squinting at

Mitch conspiratorily. Her eyes were an unusual grayish green.

"Times are tough," Mitch murmured agreeably.

Vela eyed him thoughtfully. "Nila now, she can't afford the luxury of worrying about Cherokee witches. Nila's old man ran out on her a while back. Ain't been heard from since. Not much of a loss, if you ask me. Mighty fond of his beer, and he wasn't too work brittle, either. But he kept a job about half the time, which was better than a kick in the pants. Now Nila's got two kids to support all by her lonesome. You can see why she was frantic when Thornton let her go."

Mitch nodded gravely. Vela Whittle was a gift, a gossip who had probably forgotten more dirty little secrets than most people ever knew. She snapped open a lighter and touched it to her cigarette, dropping it back into her pocket as she drew in deeply.

"You've confirmed what I've heard from several sources, that Thornton wasn't an easy man to work for," Mitch told her with a smile, to let her know how helpful she was being.

Harrumphing, she tipped her head back and blew smoke at the ceiling. "Had a hair-trigger temper. I kept out of his way."

"Did Mr. Thornton often fire employees without warning?"

"He's been known to. I heard him scream at a waiter once, in front of a dining room full of people. The waiter spilled hot coffee on a guest's shoe. No harm done really, but Mr. Thornton called him everything but a billy goat and made him leave right then. Wouldn't even let him finish out the day. I ask you, would you treat an employee like that?"

"I hope not," Mitch replied. "Do you know the waiter's name?"

"George Wilbur." She frowned. "Oh, I see why you're asking. But George didn't kill Mr. Thornton. He got a job in California. Left here six or seven months ago and hasn't been back."

"I see."

"Strange man, Mr. Thornton. He'd let some people get by with stuff. Depending on his mood. That was the thing, y'see. You never could tell what mood he'd be in."

"I'm surprised he kept any employees, in that sort of atmosphere."

"Jobs ain't that easy to find around Buckskin. Most of us can't be picky." She cackled suddenly. "Julian Moncrief now, that's a horse of a different breed. He wouldn't take any guff off Mr. Thornton."

Mitch glanced down at his list of employees. "That would be the chef."

"Studied in Paris," she confided. "La-de-da. Julian's about as high on hisself as anybody I ever saw. Snotty. Temperamental, y'know. You ask me, he's a fairy."

Mitch nudged the woman back on track. "And Mr. Thornton tolerated Julian Moncrief's—uh, temperament, when he might have fired another person."

She took a drag and blew smoke out her nose. "Julian could get by with murder."

Mitch wondered if the turn of phrase was accidental. "I would imagine that made for some resentment among the other employees."

"Sometimes. Course, we got a good laugh when Julian bragged to everybody about getting the head chef's job in a fancy Dallas hotel and then found out he didn't get it after all. He told Nila when the folks in Dallas called Mr. Thornton for a reference he lied about Julian and that's why he didn't get the job.''

"Do you think Mr. Thornton did that?''

"Wouldn't put it past him. But Julian could have made it up to save his pride. According to *him*, Mr. Thornton lied to keep him from leaving the lodge.'' She sat forward in her chair, crossing one knee over the other. Her toe drummed nervously against the desk. "In so many words, he said the Thorntons would never find another chef as good as he is.''

"Nothing like having confidence in yourself.''

She snorted and lit a new cigarette from the stub of the old. She inhaled greedily, sucking her cheeks in to form deep hollows. "That's one thing Julian don't lack.''

"By the way,'' Mitch asked offhandedly, "what time was it when you cleaned Mr. Thornton's suite Monday?''

"One o'clock,'' she answered without hesitation. "Always go in there right after lunch.''

"And how long did it take you to clean the suite?''

"No more'n thirty minutes. You get the routine down, it goes fast.''

"You cleaned all the bathroom fixtures, emptied the wastebaskets, that sort of thing?''

"Oh, yes, and changed the sheets and ran the vacuum and dusted, too. I don't do slipshod work.''

"Did you know Mr. Thornton was a diabetic?''

"Didn't everybody? I saw his insulin on the bedside table several times, when I went in to clean.''

"What about Monday? Was the insulin on the table?''

"Yes, right there beside the bed. I picked it up while I was dusting and put it back down where I found it. I know some diabetics keep it in the refrigerator, but Mr. Thornton usually kept what he was using on that bedside table. Said he didn't like to use it cold."

"Did you notice anything different about it Monday?"

She stared at him blankly. "The insulin?"

He nodded.

"Insulin is insulin, as far as I'm concerned."

"When did you go home that day?"

"After seven. Nila and I had to work overtime. Two of the maids called in sick. Then I had to wait for my brother-in-law to pick me up."

"Did you see anybody entering or leaving Graham Thornton's suite between one thirty and the time you left to go home?"

"I was busy, cleaning other rooms. There could have been a parade going in and out of there, for all I know. The only person I saw was Julian Moncrief."

"What time was this?"

"Right before my brother-in-law got here, so it must've been about seven or a little after."

"You didn't see Moncrief come out of the suite?"

"Nope. I heard 'em arguing, though, as I was leaving the lodge."

"Arguing? About what?"

She shrugged. "Couldn't say. But they were hot. I heard Moncrief say something like, 'Don't push me, Thornton,' but that's all. I didn't think too much about it. They had a riproaring argument about once a week. I think Mr. Thornton kind of enjoyed it."

Mitch stored the information and switched directions. "Do you know Magda Thornton?"

"Not very well. She didn't come around the lodge much, even before they split up. Mr. Thornton's mother never did, either, till about six months after her husband died. Then—well, I guess it was a way of keeping busy, keeping her mind off her loss."

"I don't suppose you heard what caused the Thorntons' separation?"

She tapped her foot and sighed. "Rumor has it Mr. Thornton tomcatted around on Magda. I never seen it with my own eyes, y'understand, but there's been plenty of talk. I always say, where there's smoke..."

"Did you ever hear any particular woman's name mentioned?"

She peered at him through a haze of smoke. After a moment, she said, "I wouldn't want to get nobody in trouble, not like some people I could mention. I told you I never seen anything with my own eyes."

A bit late for circumspection, Mitch thought. Too bad she hadn't waited another few minutes, though. "I assure you whatever is said in this office is confidential, Mrs. Whittle. Did you ever hear anything about a relationship between Mr. Thornton and Joy Yeaky?"

A faint flare of the grayish-green eyes told him he'd touched a nerve. "Don't remember," she mumbled. "Whyn't you ask Hazel. Her tongue's loose at both ends." The pot casting aspersions on the kettle, Mitch thought.

She stamped out her cigarette. "Can I go now? I got work to do." She'd turned stubborn, and Mitch knew he'd get nothing else from her.

"Yes. Thank you for your cooperation."

Duck watched the woman leave. "I wonder what Thornton and the chef argued about."

"We'll ask Moncrief, in due time."

"What about Thornton and Joy Yeaky? Do you really think there was something between them?"

"I don't know yet." Mitch preferred not to mention that sly flare of gray-green eyes at this stage. "But a blond woman was in Thornton's suite Monday sometime after one thirty. What time does Joy Yeaky come to work?"

"Two o'clock."

Mitch leaned back in his chair and put his hands behind his head. "Pansy Nibell and Judy Browne leave when Joy comes on. Pansy told me that sometimes a second woman works the desk with Joy, but Thornton told her not to come to work this week because business has been slow. According to Pansy, he occasionally gave one or the other of the people on the desk time off without pay, but never Joy."

"Sounds like he wanted to keep her handy."

"Could be."

"You think Larry Leaky knew about his wife and Thornton?"

"*If* there was anything to know."

"Yeah, if."

Mitch had asked himself the same question. The Yeakys had been married less than two years—practically honeymooners still. What could have possessed Joy to get tangled up with a man like Graham Thornton—*if* she was. Larry was a big, good-looking kid—he'd been a high school football star. Young and healthy and no doubt a lusty stud. The few times Mitch had seen Larry and Joy together, they'd appeared devoted to each other. And yet... appearances could be deceiving.

The Yeakys had graduated from high school three years ago last May. That'd make them about twenty-one now, nineteen when they married. Sometimes people who married young began to feel trapped, as though they'd been cheated out of sowing their wild oats. Maybe that's what had happened to Joy. Even so, what did it have to do with Thornton's murder? If Joy was sowing her wild oats with Thornton, why would she murder him? On the other hand, if her relationship with Thornton was strictly business, it would seem she'd have even less reason.

Larry Yeaky was something else. If there was hanky-panky going on and he knew it, Mitch did not find it too difficult to visualize Larry tearing out to the lodge with murder in his eye. But tampering with Thornton's insulin didn't seem like Larry's style, assuming he knew how much regular insulin to add to the NPH to kill Thornton. Not impossible, of course. Anybody could research the subject. Look it up in the library. Get a doctor or a pharmacist talking about diabetes, and they'd tell you anything you wanted to know.

But Mitch could more easily picture Larry storming into the lodge, curses and fists flying.

Maybe he could get some answers from Joy later.

"Duck, why don't you see if you can scare us up some coffee. Then ask Pansy to send in Nila Ridge."

By the time Nila entered the office hesitantly ten minutes later, Mitch had decided on an aggressive approach. She smiled uncertainly and sat down when Mitch indicated that she should do so.

While she was still settling back in the chair, Mitch said, "I understand Graham Thornton fired you."

She looked at him, her dark eyes like a startled fawn's. Mitch had not known it was possible for a full-blooded Indian's skin to become ashen, but her face did in that moment. "I see you've been talking to somebody about me. Did Julian tell you?'' She was a small woman, and she seemed to become smaller still, as though she were shrinking in upon herself.

Mitch preferred not to disabuse her of her conclusion. "I'd like to hear your version of what happened."

"It was week before last." She paused to clear her throat. She seemed not to know what to do with her hands, so she stuffed them into her uniform pockets. "I was up with Eugene—my son—the night before. He had strep throat and a high fever. I was worn out before I even came to work that morning." She halted, watching Mitch, as though trying to gauge his reaction.

"Go on."

"About eleven, I took a break. I went to the kitchen for coffee and took it into the storeroom off the pantry. I only meant to put my head down for a second...."

"You fell asleep?"

"Yes. It must've been a half hour later when Mr. Thornton came in and caught me. I tried to explain—but he was too mad to listen."

"He fired you and you went to LaDonna Thornton."

A flash of anger raked her face and left a spark in her eyes. "It wasn't fair. I've worked hard here for eighteen months, and the first time I ever wasted a minute's time on the job, he fired me." Silently Mitch agreed. "I knew Mrs. Thornton would speak to him, get him to let me stay on."

"And did she?"

"She would have. She was supposed to call me at home. But the same day I talked to her, she came down with the flu before she could do it. Then I guess she forgot. When I talked to him later—or tried to, I realized she had never said anything to him about it.''

''That would have been Monday, when you talked to him?''

It was a shot in the dark, but it struck home. She cast a brief, harried glance around the room, as though seeking an escape route. Duck was sitting in a chair beside the door, with his legs stretched out across the opening. Mitch was sure it had never occurred to Duck to block her way, but it must have seemed otherwise to Nila.

''I tried to talk to him when I finished work about six, but he was in his suite and—well, I didn't want to disturb him. So I waited out there in the reception room. When he came in—''

''What time was that?''

''Six fifteen . . . something like that.''

If Vela Whittle was right about the time she heard Thornton and Moncrief arguing, Thornton must have returned to his suite soon after Nila saw him in his office. Had he gone there to give himself the insulin injection and found Moncrief waiting for him?

''You asked him to give you another chance?''

''I begged him. He said I was wasting his time and shut the door in my face.''

''That must have been very upsetting.''

She slumped in the chair and dropped her gaze. ''Julian didn't come to work today, so you must have talked to him before you came to the lodge.'' She took a deep breath. ''If you've spoken to him, you know what happened. You know I went to the storeroom, that I talked to Julian there.'' She looked up at him defiantly. "Yes, I said I wanted to kill Graham Thornton."

Duck sat forward alertly. Mitch gave an imperceptible shake of his head.

But Nila was too caught up in her own misery to be distracted. "I was angry and I didn't know where I'd find another job, how I'd feed my kids and keep a roof over their heads. Haven't you ever been mad enough to want to kill somebody just for an instant? Haven't you ever said, 'I could kill him'? People say things like that all the time. But they don't really mean it."

Mitch tented his fingers in front of him. "Usually they don't." He looked at her, his chin resting on his fingertips. "But Graham Thornton was murdered. Somebody meant it, didn't they?"

"Well, it wasn't me! After I thought it over, I knew I'd got too upset. Mrs. Thornton would have made sure I had a job."

Mitch didn't think she'd been that confident, but he let it pass. "Thank you—" He halted, looking toward the door, at the same moment that Nila's and Duck's heads swung around. From the lobby, they heard voices raised.

Mitch pushed himself out of his chair and strode down the hall, followed by Duck and Nila. In the lobby, young Jimmy was jumping up and down, his arms flailing as he talked. "I saw it, Mommy! I'm not making it up!"

Pansy Nibell hovered over him, appearing on the verge of wringing her hands. A harried young woman in jeans and sweater, who looked as though she'd recently awakened from a nap, said, "Oh, Jimmy, I told you to stay on the sidewalk. You're tracking mud all over the carpet. Look at your hands. And those shoes! Sit down and let me take them off.''

Jimmy flopped into a chair, and his mother pulled at a shoe, transferring the mud to her hands. ''It was a head, Mommy, honest. A real head. I pulled it out of the mud.''

She tugged off the second she and held both shoes in a mud-encrusted hand. ''Maybe a cat or dog got sick and died.''

''No, it was a person's head.''

''No tall tales now, Jimmy, please. Come on, I'm putting you in the bathtub.''

Jimmy stuck his bottom lip out and shook his head. Mitch stepped forward. ''Ma'am, may I ask Jimmy a question?''

She stared at Mitch's badge and blinked. ''Why, yes, I guess so.''

Mitch squatted down in front of the boy. ''Jimmy, where did you see this head?''

''Out there.'' Jimmy gestured toward the glass at the back of the lobby. ''In those trees.'' He cocked his head and studied Mitch. ''You believe me?''

''Yes, I do, son. I'm a policeman, and I'm going right now to investigate.''

''Wow!'' Jimmy threw his mother an I-told-you-so smirk. ''Can I go, too?''

''You'd better go along with your mother.''

Mitch straightened and gestured for Duck. ''Let's go check it out.'' In the background, Jimmy was complaining mightily as his mother dragged him out of the lobby.

They had no trouble following Jimmy's route into the woods, which started about two hundred yards in back of the lodge. His footprints were clearly visible in ground still mushy from melted snow.

A dozen yards into the woods, a rotted tree trunk had fallen across a small clearing, churning up earth along its length and exposing the top of a human skull. Jimmy had dug down next to it, enough to identify it for what it was. The eye sockets stared dolefully at the intruders.

"Lord have mercy," Duck breathed. "Another murder."

"I doubt it," Mitch said, "but we'll probably never know for sure. The body has been buried here for years."

"Who could it be?"

"I don't know who, but my guess is it was a Chero- kee."

Duck's mismatched eyes were as round as coat but- tons. "The Indian graveyard!" He looked around leerily. "Must be other bodies buried here, too. We could be standing on 'em." He retreated a few steps. "Let's get outa here, Chief."

They walked back toward the lodge. "You talk to the security guard," Mitch said. He had just remembered that he'd agreed, a week ago, to meet Lisa for lunch today. "Tell him to rope off that clearing and keep people out. Then we'll go back to town and I'll call my cousin, Callie Roach."

Duck looked at him blankly.

"Callie's active in the Cherokee Historical Society. I think they'll want to restore the site, put up a fence and a marker. Maybe their research will turn up the names of the people buried out there."

Duck glanced over his shoulder. "Good thing we ain't nervous types."

"Nervous?"

"The type to see the supernatural in everything that happens."

"Ghosts, you mean."

"Not that I believe in that nonsense, o' course."

"Of course."

"Still," Duck mused, "it's mighty odd, Graham Thornton dying outside the lodge and so close to those woods, with all the rumors that have been going around—about the lodge being on an Indian grave-yard and Cherokee witches being upset about it."

"Duck, it wasn't a witch who tinkered with Thornton's insulin."

"I know that," Duck said a bit huffily. "I'm just saying it's strange."

Mitch nodded, reflecting that Duck wouldn't be the only one to remark upon the coincidence.

IT WAS NOON. Mitch and Lisa Macpherson occupied a booth in the Three Squares Cafe on Highway 10. Last week they'd agreed to meet at Judy's, a roadhouse on the lake road outside of Buckskin. It was one place where they could be fairly sure of not running into somebody from the high school or one of Emily's friends.

Remembering there was no longer any reason to hide, Mitch had intercepted Lisa before she left the high school and changed the meeting place. The Three Squares was more convenient for both of them.

Before leaving the lodge, he had tried to arrange a meeting with Julian Moncrief during the afternoon, but when he called Moncrief's home number, he got a recorded message. He hung up without leaving his name. Moncrief rented a house in Lakeview, the community not far from the lodge. After he returned to the station, Mitch would try again to get hold of Moncrief.

He'd dropped off Duck at the station before partially retracing his route to meet Lisa. It had been six days since they'd seen each other. To Mitch it seemed longer.

She looked lovely in a pink sweater with a lacy collar and small silver heart earrings. Her shoulder-length blond hair glistened with trapped sunshine in the light streaming through the café's windows.

He was about to tell her what a fine-looking woman she was when Geraldine Duckworth came out of the kitchen to take their order. Geraldine was a short, chunky woman. Her brown hair was covered by a net. She came toward them, smiling.

"Hey, you two. It's good to see you in here together."

Geraldine had to have heard by now about the problem Mitch was having with Emily. Before she could ask how that was going, he said, "I'm worried about Duck, Geraldine. He's not losing that weight. I made a policy, and I'm going to have to stick by it."

She nodded. "I know. I keep telling him he'd better get with it."

"You're a smart woman," Mitch said. "Can't you do something to help him?"

"I already told him, when he eats in here from now on, he's getting the light menu." She took out her order pad. "I'll give it some more thought, though. It wouldn't hurt me to lose a few pounds, either. Now, what'll it be?"

They ordered cheeseburger baskets. As soon as they were alone, Mitch said, "I missed you." He reached for her hand beneath the table.

"Really?" she asked; a bit too brightly, he thought. She pulled her hand away and glanced around. "Are you going to tell me why we're so bold, all of a sudden—sitting here at high noon in the middle of town?"

He pulled a paper napkin from the dispenser. "How's Emily doing in your English class?"

She eyes him reflectively. "Her work's fine. But, all of a sudden, she doesn't talk to me. Comes in the door as the bell is ringing and scoots out afterward ahead of the crowd."

"She found out about us."

Looking down, she toyed with her fork. "I guessed that was it. So now she resents me."

"Both of us. She says I'm being disloyal to Ellen's memory. Kid talk."

"Is it, Mitch? Sometimes, I wonder if you don't agree with Emily about that."

"I thought we picked that particular bone a long time ago." When Mitch had first tried to date Lisa last September, she'd said he hadn't yet dealt with his loss. He'd managed to convince her otherwise.

"So did I."

"Emily's still a child in a lot of ways. She's at a difficult age. She'll come around."

She looked up at him, holding his gaze. "In the meantime?"

"We ignore her sulks. I haven't even been able to have a satisfying conversation with her about us yet. She's involved in all that stuff at school, and now she's in the middle of semester tests. I've been busy, too. There's been a murder out at the lodge."

"Another murder?" She was thinking of the double murder case the department had been investigating in September, when they met. "Imagine, I thought I was coming to a hotbed of peace and tranquility when I moved to Buckskin. I expected to be bored...then you came along."

"And got struck by lightning the first time I saw you."

Her expression remained grave. "When I didn't hear from you all week, I thought you were having second thoughts—about us."

"You know better than that."

She didn't say whether she did or not. After a brief pause, she changed the subject. "Who was the murder victim?"

Mitch told her what he'd learned, knowing he could depend on her to keep it to herself. She was a good listener, and it was nice to have somebody not involved in the case to bounce his thoughts off of.

They shared a piece of carrot cake for dessert. The time with Lisa was relaxing, and Mitch was sorry to see it end. Outside, he put his arm around her and walked her to her Honda. "Mitch," she said, "I'm glad Emily knows about us. I'm tired of sneaking around. It makes me feel like a teenager, slipping off to see someone her parents disapprove of."

He kissed her nose.

"Only," she went on thoughtfully, "I wish you'd been the one to tell her."

He kissed her mouth lightly. "Can I see you tonight? Emily's planning to spend the night with Temple Roberts. I think she'd like to move in over there if she could."

He knew immediately he shouldn't have added the part about Emily. It had sounded as though he only wanted to see Lisa when Emily had other plans, but he hadn't meant it that way.

She touched his cheek. Her eyes clouded. "Let's cool it for a few days, until you and Emily can reach an understanding."

He wanted to argue, but her expression stayed his tongue. She got into her blue Honda Civic and he watched her drive away. He went to the Land Cruiser and waited for a cortege to pass. It was led by the Buckskin Funeral Home's black limousine, carrying the Thornton family to Graham Thornton's funeral.

EIGHT

MITCH SWUNG BY the Yeaky house, hoping to catch Joy before she left for work. No one was at home. Back at the station, he looked up Julian Moncrief's phone number and dialed. He got the recording again and this time left a message for Moncrief to call him back.

Later that afternoon, Mitch was pumping hard on his exercise bike when a warbly female voice announced, "Chief Bushyhead, we have some information about your murder case."

Mitch jerked his head up. Millicent and Polly Kirkwood stood in the open office doorway in prim, dark dresses and black orthopedic shoes, their gray hair bound in tight buns at their napes. Millicent was tall and rail thin. Small, rimless spectacles perched on her nose. Polly was shorter and plumper, and she had fat naturally pink cheeks. The description "apple-cheeked" seemed to have been coined especially for her. When Mitch thought of Polly, he pictured her wearing an apron and taking cookies from the oven. He could more easily envision Millicent in a classroom, where she had spent forty years of her life, rapping a disruptive student's knuckles with her ruler.

"Come in, ladies." Mitch grabbed the towel looped over the handlebar and wiped the sweat off his face. "Sit down." He'd removed his shirt while he exercised and now put it on over his damp T-shirt, having caught the disapproval in Millicent's tight-pursed lips.

"We expected to leave a message for you, naturally assuming you'd be out investigating the heinous crime that has been committed in our midst," Millicent said, settling in her chair. She planted her black oxfords firmly together and smoothed her dress modestly over her knees.

Since few things remained secret for long in Buckskin, Mitch was not surprised to learn the sisters had already heard that Graham Thornton's death was being investigated as a murder.

"You mustn't blame that nice young Officer Stephens," Polly chirped, lighting beside her sister. Like two wrens on a perch. "We heard about poor Mr. Thornton at the grocery store. Officer Stephens didn't say a word about the case to us. Such a fine boy."

Mitch had been sure of that, since Roo had left for the Kirkwoods' house that morning before Mitch talked to the medical examiner. "Officer Stephens will be pleased to know you think so highly of him, Miss Polly."

"Well, aren't you going to ask us for our information?" Millicent demanded, obviously thinking none too highly of Mitch's handling of the Thornton case.

"I was about to, Miss Millicent."

She sniffed. "You'll want to write this down."

Clamping down on his impatience, Mitch moved some papers around on his desk until he found a pen and memo pad. "Ready."

Miss Polly leaned forward and whispered, "It was him."

"He, Polly," Millicent corrected, ever the English instructor.

"That's what I said. It was him."

"No," Millicent sighed, as though she despaired of ever teaching her sister the proper use of her native tongue. "The correct construction is, 'It was he.'"

"Fiddlesticks. Chief Bushyhead knows what I mean."

"Not really, Miss Polly," Mitch said. "Who are you referring—" Millicent tut-tutted and he corrected himself. "To whom are you referring?"

"Why, our despicable housebreaker, of course. He's the murderer."

Since Millicent was staring at him, Mitch wrote "housebreaker" on the memo pad, refraining with difficulty from adding "imaginary" before the word. "What makes you think so?"

"Because he tried to break in Monday night."

Unable to see a connection where none existed, Mitch cleared his throat noncommittally.

Millicent pushed her rimless spectacles up her nose with an index finger. "We were at home. Don't you understand?" She might as well have added "you pathetic excuse for a homicide investigator." It was written on her face. "He's never before tried to gain admittance while we were on the premises. It proves he's become quite desperate, wouldn't you say?"

Polly's blue-veined hand plucked at her lace collar as she nodded emphatic agreement. "We suspect he's a dope fiend. There are so many of them nowadays. One almost fears leaving the house. And now, even there, we aren't safe."

Mitch sighed. "Did you get a look at him?"

"Only his footprints," Millicent said. "But we heard him. He circled the house, rattling windows." Mitch didn't bother to remind them that there had been a strong wind Monday night. They wouldn't accept such a mundane explanation for their rattling windows.

"Our phone was out of order, so we couldn't call for help," Polly said.

"I told Polly we must be brave. It was up to us to protect ourselves."

"We are being forced to sink to the level of violence in self-defense," Polly continued. "Millicent armed herself with a poker, and I filled a spray bottle with Clorox, fully prepared to aim for his eyes if he came in. I expect it would have blinded him."

"I suppose the footprints were gone by morning," Mitch said.

Millicent peered over her spectacles and down her pointed nose at him. "Of course. That was the night we had the eleven-inch snow."

Mitch shook his head. "Too bad. But why do you think he left your house and murdered Graham Thornton?" He couldn't believe he was talking to the sisters as though he took their housebreaker story seriously. But maybe it was the easiest way. Let them have their little moment of self-importance, say he'd look into it, and hustle them out of his office.

"We've just explained that," Millicent said, clearly exasperated with his slow uptake. "He's desperate. He must need money for his dope. I imagine he left our house, mad with rage because his dastardly plan had been thwarted. In his frenzy, perhaps he drove around and picked a victim at random. In which case, poor Mr. Thornton had the unfortunate luck to be in the wrong place at the wrong time."

"Graham Thornton wasn't robbed," Mitch said.

"A dope fiend doesn't think like you and me," Polly interjected knowingly. "His powers of reason have been damaged by chemicals."

"But if your housebreaker didn't need money for drugs..."

"We're merely pointing out possibilities," Millicent said.

"I don't think he chose his victim at random. I think he chose Mr. Thornton particularly," Polly said.

"Why?"

Millicent squinted at him. "Ferreting out his motive is your job, Chief Bushyhead. I would simply remind you of what Mark Twain said: 'Everyone is a moon, and has a dark side which he never shows to anybody.' You can be sure that Graham Thornton was no exception. Find that dark side, and it will lead you to the murderer."

Mitch scribbled a few meaningless words on his pad and slipped it out of sight beneath a folder. "Well, this certainly gives me a new avenue to explore. I appreciate your coming forward."

"Any civic-minded citizen would have done the same," Millicent told him. "We are always happy to cooperate with the police."

"Indeed," agreed Polly.

Mitch levered himself out of his chair. It squeaked loudly. "I'd better get right on it. Thank you for coming by, ladies." He ushered them out of the station.

"A hot tip on the Thornton case?" Helen asked as the door shut behind the sisters.

"How'd you guess?"

"They told me they had some information about the case. Wouldn't say what it was, though. It was for your ears only. What was the tip?"

"A quotation from Mark Twain, no less."

"Gee, I'm impressed."

Mitch chuckled. Now that the sisters were gone, it was easier to see the humor in their fixation on their housebreakers. He went back to his office and phoned Julian Moncrief. He got the recorded message again. Was Moncrief out or simply not answering his phone? Before calling it a day, he decided to drive out to the man's house to be sure, then stop at the lodge and interview Joy Yeaky.

MONCRIEF WAS NOT at home. The house was locked and shuttered, and there was no car in the garage. Mitch had an anxious moment, wondering if the chef had flown the coop. Then he told himself that Moncrief couldn't feel threatened since he hadn't been questioned yet. From what Vela Whittle had said, Moncrief had a healthy ego. If he had murdered Graham Thornton, he probably wouldn't believe a small-town cop was smart enough to pin it on him. He'd be back. Mitch returned to the Land Cruiser and drove to the lodge.

He expected to see Joy Yeaky at the registration desk. Instead, he found Pansy Nibell, who informed Mitch, "I'm working the first half of Joy's shift and another employee is taking the last half. The overtime pay will come in handy for Christmas bills." Her chin wobbled. She seemed happy to see him.

"Is Joy sick?"

Pansy hesitated, but only for an instant. "She didn't say, but she didn't sound sick. Between you and me, she may be looking for another job. Finding Mr. Thornton like that—it really shook her up. I think she'd prefer never to see the lodge again."

Moncrief and now Joy. Mitch was getting the distinct impression that people were avoiding him. "How about if I buy you a cup of coffee, Pansy?"

"Oh, my." Flustered, she patted her hair. "Well, I might be able to get one of the waiters to sit at the desk while I'm gone."

"Good."

"Let me check." She picked up the phone, talked to somebody, and hung up. "I told them it was police business. Someone's coming out to relieve me."

It was Billy Choate who came. Mitch was rather surprised to see him. He'd expected Billy to quit, for fear of being the next victim of the night walker. Billy hadn't arrived for work yet when Mitch and Duck were there that morning.

"When Mrs. Nibell and I get back, I'd like to ask you some questions, Billy," Mitch said.

He didn't look thrilled about it.

The dining room was cedar-beamed with cedar-framed windows along one wall, looking out on evergreen shrubbery and big clay pots for summer flowers. A narrow cobblestone walk wound among them. Bright-colored patchwork quilts decorated the other three walls. A few couples were eating an early dinner.

"If there's a dinner rush, it won't be until about seven," Pansy said, leading the way to a corner table. "We can talk here."

Mitch said nothing more until a waiter poured their coffee. "Pansy, I'm going to tell you something in confidence because I know I can trust you."

She flushed with excitement. "Oh, my. You can certainly count on me, Chief."

Mitch stirred cream into his coffee. "I have reason to believe that Graham Thornton and Joy Yeaky were having an affair."

She glanced around surreptitiously to assure herself that they weren't being overheard. She planted her fat, dimpled elbows on the table and leaned closer. "Who told you that?"

"I can't reveal my sources. I'm sure you understand."

"Oh. Of course." She picked up her napkin and blotted her brow. "Well, I know it wasn't Vela. Joy's mother and Vela are first cousins. So it must have been Hazel or Nila."

Ah ha, Mitch thought. Vela Whittle's uncharacteristic circumspection when he questioned her about Joy was now explained. He sipped his coffee and waited.

"Have you asked Joy about it?"

"Not yet."

She dumped four packets of sugar in her coffee and stirred distractedly. "I wouldn't want her to know we'd talked."

"As I said, I protect my sources."

She chewed her bottom lip. "I do want to help with your investigation. It's not as though I'd be telling you something you don't already know." She picked up her coffee, blew on it, took a swallow, set it down. The cup rattled against the saucer.

Mitch's conscience pricked him, but he ignored it. "That's true."

Pansy seemed to be having a struggle with her own conscience, but she won it quickly. "Joy's not really a bad girl. She's just young and careless. I don't think she's learned yet that you have to take responsibility for the choices you make. You have to pay the price."

On the contrary, Mitch reflected, Joy might have recently learned that lesson very well. "When did the affair start?"

She picked up her spoon and stared at it unseeingly. "I don't know. I first heard talk about it among the employees two or three months ago." She dropped the spoon and took another swallow of coffee.

"It's common knowledge then?"

"There have been a lot of rumors. How much fact is behind them, I can't say."

"This isn't an official interrogation, Pansy. Give me your impressions."

She set her cup down. "Mr. Thornton and his wife were separated. He was living here, as you know. After five or six o'clock, there's often not much to do at the registration desk." She looked up at Mitch almost beseechingly. "He was always around, you see, and Joy had time on her hands. I imagine she thought of it as a lark in the beginning."

"And later?"

She frowned. "In the last month, she's seemed—oh, tense, edgy. That was my impression, at any rate. I didn't see that much of her, of course."

"Do you think she broke off with Thornton?"

"I think—well, she may have wanted to, but she didn't quite know how. She was out of her depth. Maybe Mr. Thornton wanted her to leave Larry. I'm not sure. I just sensed that Joy was troubled. Larry's in school full-time. Joy has to work, so she would have been concerned about keeping her job." She pondered for a moment. "I think it was only a matter of time until she'd have had to quit, though. I don't see how she could have continued working for him. Now, after what's happened, it must be more unpleasant for her here than before."

"How do you mean?"

She shook her head. "I'd had a lot of silly thoughts on the matter. Nothing I know for sure."

"I'd like to hear what you think."

"Well, if Joy wanted out and Mr. Thornton didn't, that might have put her in a real bind."

It certainly might have, Mitch thought.

"Mr. Thornton was a prideful man. And he was vengeful. If Joy hurt him—humiliated him, he could have been angry enough to hurt her back. He wouldn't have simply let it go. Mr. Thornton wasn't the type to forgive and forget. In a situation like that, a person might think about what a relief it would be if the other person just wasn't *there*, anymore. Do you see what I mean?"

Mitch saw plenty. All speculation, alas. But he hadn't read her mind, after all. "If Joy had thoughts like that and then found Mr. Thornton dead in *her* car," she continued, "how could she help but feel guilty? As though she'd wished him dead. That's why I think she's looking for another job. To stay here would be a constant reminder."

Had it never occurred to Pansy Nibell that Joy might have done more than *wish* Thornton dead?

She gave him a bright smile. "Mercy, how I do run on. My husband says I should have been a writer, with my imagination."

"I'm sure you'd have been a fine writer."

She glanced at her watch, suddenly anxious to get away. Her conscience was battling back. She was regretting saying so much. "I'd better get back to the desk." Mitch thanked her and said he'd wait in the dining room for Billy.

The interview with Choate was disappointing. The young man was reticent and a bit suspicious. He told Mitch as little as possible, and nothing Mitch didn't already know.

When Mitch got home, Temple Roberts was there with Emily. It was Temple who came into the living room to greet him. "Hi, Chief Bushyhead."

Mitch ruffled her red curls fondly. Temple's big blue eyes gave her an expression of perpetual surprise. "Hiya, kid. What's up?"

"We're about ready to go over to my house."

"I'll drive you."

"Great!"

"Big plans for this evening?"

Temple grinned. "Kevin and his cousin, who's visiting from Tahlequah, are coming over. We're going to make popcorn and watch a Dirty Harry movie."

Dirty Harry. Whatever happened to John Wayne? Mitch wondered. Emily came down the stairs carrying her overnight bag. "Hi, sweetheart," Mitch said.

"Hi, Daddy." She smiled a bit wanly. She didn't turn away or grimace when he kissed her. Mitch felt reassured. She was going to be all right, he told himself.

After making dinner and eating it alone, Mitch tried to watch a television talk show, but he couldn't keep his mind on the inane chatter of four teenage film actors, who comprised the panel for the evening. Finally he switched off the set and sat in his living room, turning over in his mind the information he'd collected during the day's investigation. He didn't put on a light, not even the Christmas-tree bulbs. He thought that the absence of visual distractions might sharpen his concentration.

Mitch toyed with the idea of money as motive. Money had been behind many a murder. At least three people connected in some way to Graham Thornton were better off financially with Thornton out of the picture.

Thornton had been in charge of his sister's trust fund, and from what Mitch had overheard in Cara's phone conversation with the lawyer, Thornton had kept a tight grip on the purse strings. It had sounded as though Cara wanted to drop out of school and travel abroad, using money from the fund, and Graham had refused to allow it. It had also sounded as though Cara had assumed the money would be turned over to her, now that her tightfisted brother was dead. From her end of the phone conversation, it seemed she'd been mistaken. But she wouldn't have known that when she tampered with the insulin, if Cara was the one who did it.

Arrangements for the trust now, of course, would depend on the trust document Oscar Thornton had drawn up before his death. That would probably be explained fully on Monday when the family gathered for the reading of Graham's will. Mitch decided he wanted to be present at that meeting.

As for Magda Thornton, she was now presumably a wealthy woman, since she was still Graham's legal wife when he died. Further, Graham's death conveniently eliminated lengthy wrangling over the divorce settlement, which Graham, if determined, could have drawn out for months, even years.

Nila Ridge had gained less, on the face of it, than either Cara or Magda by Graham's death. But everything was relative. To Nila, losing her job could well have been more devastating than Cara's inability to get at her trust fund money or the possibility that Magda's divorce settlement might have been less than generous. Nila had two children to support, few skills, and no husband to help her.

The financial circumstances of all three women gave them reason to wish Graham Thornton out of the way. Did one of them leave off wishing and resort to murder?

If Graham Thornton wasn't killed because of money, what was left? Revenge? Thornton had lied to keep Julian Moncrief from leaving the lodge, if the chef's story could be believed. But that hardly seemed a motive for murder. If Moncrief was as talented as he apparently thought, he could have found another job somewhere, though admittedly it would have been difficult without a reference.

That brought him to Joy Yeaky. Was fear the motive? Fear of being harmed or exposed in some way? Mitch was now convinced that Joy was the blond woman in Thornton's suite Monday afternoon. And what was it Pansy Nibel had said? *If Joy wanted out and Mr. Thornton didn't, that might have put her in a real bind.*

When Mitch left work that afternoon, he'd had every intention of postponing further interrogations until Monday, unless something new developed. But as the evening lengthened, he couldn't stop thinking about the case. He got up from his chair and turned on a light. Going to the telephone, he looked up the Yeakys' number and dialed. Joy answered.

"This is Mitch Bushyhead, Joy. I'd like to talk to you."

"What about?" She had lowered her voice.

"Graham Thornton's murder."

There was a soft intake of breath. "This is a really bad time for me."

"Is Larry there?"

"Yes."

"Perhaps I could talk to both of you together."

"No! You can't come here. I—I'll meet you somewhere."

"When?"

"Whenever you say. Just don't come here."

"Tonight?"

"All right, but I can't be gone long."

"The police station?"

"Oh, no. Uh—let me think. You know that empty building on First Street? It used to be a grocery store."

"I know it."

"I'll meet you there, in back. Fifteen minutes." She hung up.

DRIVING DOWN SEQUOYAH, Mitch saw a woman come out of the phone booth next to the post office. She pulled her coat collar up, a furtive gesture, and walked quickly to the corner of Sequoyah and Pawnee streets, where she turned west. A street lamp illuminated her face for an instant and Mitch recognized Nila Ridge. He stopped his car at the corner and watched her. She walked west on Pawnee for a block and got into a car parked at the curb. Didn't she have a telephone at home? And why had she parked so far from the phone booth?

Curious, Mitch checked his watch and saw he had ten minutes before he was due to meet Joy Yeaky. He followed Nila, keeping a block or two behind her. She drove straight to her house, which appeared to have a light on in every room, got out, and went inside.

For a moment, Mitch debated whether to go to the house and talk to Nila. Her odd secretiveness in leaving the phone booth was stuck in his mind. He was sure she had a telephone. During his interview with Nila at the lodge, she'd mentioned that before LaDonna fell ill she'd promised to talk to Graham about Nila's employment and phone Nila "at home."

Nila had used the public pay phone because she didn't want to be overheard. That, combined with her anxiety when he'd questioned her, made Mitch wonder. If he knew whom she'd called and what was said, would the information aid in the murder investigation?

He was tempted to knock on Nila's door and try to find out, but if he did he'd be late for the appointment with Joy Yeaky. Besides, there could be a dozen reasons why she might not have wanted to use the telephone at home. Maybe she'd wanted to talk in confidence to a friend and didn't want to be overheard. Maybe she'd tracked her husband down and didn't want her children to know until she'd talked to him. Whatever her reason, it could wait, he decided.

Afterward, Mitch remembered that moment of indecision very clearly. As he drove away from Nila Ridge's house, he had a strong feeling that he should go back. But Joy probably wouldn't have waited for him. He continued driving to the abandoned building on First Street. Joy Yeaky seemed more likely than Nila Ridge to possess knowledge pertinent to Graham Thornton's murder.

Although he could not know what had been set in motion that night or how terrible the repercussions, Mitch would always wonder how subsequent events might have been altered if he'd heeded his feelings and gone back.

NINE

SHE WAS ALREADY THERE when Mitch pulled around behind the abandoned building. There was a square, blacktopped area surrounded by a sagging fence. No one around at night for blocks. Joy had chosen the ideal place for a meeting she wanted kept secret. Mitch wondered why she'd thought of it. Had she come there to meet Graham Thornton?

She left her car, came over to the Land Cruiser, and got in.

"I have to be home by eight," she said immediately. "I told Larry I was returning some borrowed books to a girlfriend. I said I wouldn't be gone long." The building cut off the light from the streetlamps. In the darkness, Mitch could see the blurred suggestion of her profile, but he couldn't make out her expression.

"Why didn't you want to talk to me in front of Larry?"

"This has nothing to do with him."

"Are you sure about that?" He felt her tension coil a little tighter and knew that she was looking at him now, trying to see his face. He had her full attention.

"Larry doesn't know anything about Graham Thornton. He never even met the man."

"Maybe he knows more about him than you think."

"Chief Bushyhead, what are you trying to say?" Her voice was uneven, the voice of a woman who had nearly reached the limit of the pressure she could tolerate without breaking.

"Did Larry know Graham Thornton was having an affair with his wife?"

"*What?* Why, that's—that's just silly!" He could tell from the tone that she was terrified and would probably crumble under the slightest pressure. He had no choice.

Mitch sighed. "Joy, we found a tissue with lipstick the color of yours on it and a long blond hair in the bathroom of Thornton's suite Monday night. We can get a comparative analysis if we have to. A good lab can determine if two hairs came from the same head."

She stared at him for another instant, then bowed her head and started crying. Mitch felt like a worm. For several moments, the only sound was Joy Yeaky's sobbing and snuffling. Mitch pulled out his handkerchief and offered it to her. "I'm sorry. I hate this as much as you do."

"Oh, I doubt that." She took the handkerchief and pressed it against her eyes. "How did you know?"

"You don't think it's any big secret out at the lodge, do you?"

She snuffled some more, then blew her nose. "I guess I hoped so. Dumb of me, I know. I've been really stupid about this whole thing."

"Were you in Thornton's suite Monday afternoon?"

She gulped air. "I went there to tell him it was over, but he—he didn't want to talk. Graham could be so hardheaded. I told him anyway. I'd wanted to end it for weeks, but I was afraid I'd lose my job. I hoped I could—well, sort of ease out of it, you know. But Monday, after the way he acted, I knew it wasn't going to be that simple. I decided to start looking for another job right away, and I told him I couldn't see him again."

"How did he take it?"

She made a hiccuping sound and bent forward in the seat, turning away from him. After a few seconds, she said, "He didn't like it. He said *he'd* decide when it was over."

"And?"

"He left the suite and I went back to work."

"I mean, what did you intend to do about what he said? Did you think you could get another job and that would be the end of it?"

"It would've had to be," she said, her voice muffled by the handkerchief. "It made me sick for him to even touch me. I really couldn't do it anymore. I told him so in no uncertain terms."

"From what I've heard about Graham Thornton, he wouldn't have let it go at that. Did you think he would?"

She expelled a long breath. "Chief Bushyhead, I don't know. I was going to take it one day at a time and get another job as fast as possible. What else could I do?"

Get him out of your life permanently, Mitch thought.

"Once I found another job," she was saying, "and didn't have to be around him anymore, I hoped he'd find somebody else. I really do love my husband."

She paused, but Mitch did not respond. It wasn't that he doubted her love for Larry. But it wasn't his job to point out that love required continual tending to keep it alive. If she didn't know that now, words wouldn't make the difference.

"I must have been crazy to get mixed up with Graham in the first place."

"Why did you?"

"I'm still not sure. For one thing, Larry had lost his job and was grouchy all the time because he couldn't find something else. Finally he decided to go to welding school and things got better. But, anyway, there I was, trying to support us and I started feeling—well, kind of sorry for myself, I guess. I don't know what made me think fooling around with Graham would make anything better. I honestly don't."

Mitch pinched the bridge of his nose and closed his eyes. He thought that if Ellen had ever had an affair, he would have sensed it. "Do you really think Larry never suspected?"

She turned her head to peer at him intently. "I'm sure of it. I'd have known. When Larry's hurt or angry, he lets you know about it. With Larry, everything is out on the table. He hates dishonesty. If he ever finds out about Graham—" She drew in an unsteady breath and pulled her coat closer around her. "You aren't going to tell Larry, are you, Chief?"

"If I have to question him—"

"But there's no need for that," she said urgently. "I told you, he doesn't know anything about Graham's death." She gripped Mitch's arm, her fingers digging in. "If you start asking Larry questions about Graham, he'll figure out why." She was crying again, her words jerking out. "Please, Chief, don't do it. If Larry ever finds out about Graham, he'll leave me. I couldn't take that."

Mitch prided her fingers off his arm. "Calm down, Joy. I won't talk to Larry if I don't have to." Didn't she know Larry was probably going to find out sooner or later? Too many people in Buckskin knew about the affair. But Mitch didn't have the heart to say that to Joy Yeaky. Let her indulge in wishful thinking as long as she could. She was about to come apart as it was.

She slumped back against the seat. "Oh, thank you." She wiped her eyes. "I was lucky this time, wasn't I? I learned my lesson, too. I'll never mess around behind Larry's back again."

Mitch stared out the window into the darkness. He hoped it wasn't a lesson learned too late. "Do you know how Graham Thornton died?"

She was silent for the space of a few seconds. "I heard there was something wrong with his insulin, that it was contaminated or something."

"When you were in Thornton's suite Monday, did you touch the insulin?"

He left her staring at him. "If I did, do you think I'd admit it?" She tossed his balled handkerchief onto the dash. "I saw it on the bedside table, but I didn't touch it. I'd swear that on the Bible."

"You may have to," Mitch told her.

He felt her shock in the ensuing silence. "You mean, I could be called to testify? They might ask me about my relationship with Graham?"

"That could happen, if the case gets to court."

"Oh, no..." She pressed the heels of her hands to her eyes. "One foolish mistake, and you have to pay and pay. Why is life so unfair?"

"Maybe it's better in the long run if Larry knows. Secrets between a husband and wife have a way of getting bigger and more important the longer they're kept."

"You don't know Larry. Even if he could forgive me, it would never be the same again."

"It's possible you aren't giving him enough credit."
Mitch had no idea whether she was or not. He simply
wanted to say something comforting. She seemed so
desperately vulnerable. If Joy Yeaky turned out to be
the murderer, he was going to hate arresting her.

She did not respond.

"You'd better leave. It's five of eight."

Without a word, she opened the door and got out.
Mitch waited until she drove away before he started his
engine. He drove back down Sequoyah, glancing at the
empty phone booth beside the post office as he passed.
Nila. Joy. Magda. Cara. Four women who had hated
Graham Thornton and whose lives would be much
easier with him in the ground. And then there was Julian Moncrief. Monday, he'd track down the chef—
after the reading of Graham Thornton's will.

TEN

Saturday, December 16

SATURDAY NIGHT, bored and restless after Emily left with Kevin to see a movie, Mitch drove past Lisa's apartment on Oak Street. He would stop, go inside, and make her talk to him. She had frightened him yesterday, saying they should cool it for a while. Had she really meant that she was cooling off about the relationship? When he tried to be objective, he knew that it might happen any time. He was ten years older than Lisa. She was getting her master's degree and wanted to go on for her doctorate. A teacher with those credentials would be crazy to stay in Buckskin. She could go into administration in a large city. More money and more challenge. He tried to imagine his life without her, the way it had been before—after Ellen died. Grief had nearly killed him, too. Lisa had given him reason to believe in life again.

Lisa. He wondered what he felt for her. Was it love? He didn't know, but he wasn't ready to call it that yet. All he did know was that the last three months had held some joy and laughter because of her.

Her windows, above the garage, were dark. Seeing them, he felt an aching regret deep inside, like a tiny fissure opening. He drove slowly by, glancing back to get a look at the side window of her bedroom, but it was as dark as the others. Where was she? It was too early for her to be asleep. Was she with another man?

That little crack deep inside him let out an ugly stream of jealousy. You are pathetic, Bushyhead. You don't own her.

Besides, she could be spending the evening with a female friend.

Hang onto that thought, Bushyhead.

ELEVEN

Sunday, December 17

MITCH WENT BACK to Lisa's apartment Sunday afternoon. Like a homing pigeon, he thought. No matter where you release him, he flies straight to home base. But his home was on Pawnee Street with Emily. The white Victorian house that Ellen had decorated so lovingly.

On this cold, dreary Sunday afternoon, he wished he could move Lisa into his house so that it would feel like home again. Pack her things up and cart them a few blocks across town. Simple and easy. Only it wasn't easy at all.

She didn't seem surprised to see him. She admitted him without a word. The apartment was warm and cluttered with books, as usual. The familiar spicy scent of the potpourri she had scattered about was somehow reassuring. He remembered the first time he had come there, the first time he had kissed her. They had ended up in her bed.

She closed the door and leaned back against it. "Well," she said.

"I couldn't stay away."

"Where is Emily?"

"There was a youth meeting at church."

"Oh."

"Does that mean I can't stay? I would have come, regardless of Emily. I came last night, but the apartment was dark."

A flicker of a smile passed over her lips. "I went out with Janet Harden. Just the two of us."

Warmth loosened the grip of the tightness inside him. How could something so simple as hearing she'd spent last evening with the high school art teacher create such a glow?

"I want to touch you," he said. "I need to."

"Oh, Mitch..."

He put his arms around her and held her against his cold clothing, inhaling the scent of her hair and feeling her soft hand at the nape of his neck.

She stepped away from him. "You feel like a block of ice. Take off your coat and let me make some hot tea."

He shed the coat and followed her into the kitchen. She put the kettle on the stove.

He cupped her chin in his hand and drew her to him. He kissed the soft mouth, devoid of lipstick, moving his lips upward to her eyelids, feeling her warm breath on his face.

She leaned against him for an instant. "Maybe," she said softly, "I'll make the tea later."

"Please."

She set the kettle off the fire and turned back into his arms.

TWELVE

Monday, December 18

DEWEY DUNLAP'S lifeless monotone ceased. He laid the will on his desk and clasped his hands on top of it. Looking up, he blinked owlishly at the three women lined up on the other side of the desk. The lawyer looked grayer than usual today, his skin a bare shade lighter than his sparse hair. Mitch wondered if the pallor came from the dread Dunlap was bound to have felt about reading Graham Thornton's last will and testament to the three women before him.

The office was small, cramped. It smelled of dust and age. The carpet was so old it was impossible to tell what its original color had been.

Mitch and Roo sat against the wall. Roo was taking notes. Mitch had been watching the three women. LaDonna Thornton was pale in a black dress, but she had remained composed during the reading, her blue-veined hands folded in her lap. Magda wore beige, not black, and Mitch had noticed a heightened color in her face as the contents of the will were revealed. She might have been fairly certain she knew what the terms were, but there had always been the chance that Graham had changed everything in the last few months. Except for the slight flush, Mitch saw no sign that she was elated or even surprised. But then, as Sullivan had said, Magda possessed extraordinary self-control.

It was Cara Thornton whose reaction was animated, as anyone who knew anything about the situation would have expected. She stared at Dunlap, after he set the will aside, stunned briefly into muteness. But she recovered herself quickly, shot out of her chair, and wheeled on Magda.

"What did you do with it?" she demanded shrilly.

Magda, perfectly groomed and regal as always, looked up at her sister-in-law with a long-suffering expression. The layers of her red hair shifted and floated back into place whenever she moved. "With what?"

"The other will!" She pointed a finger at the document on the desk. "That one was made three months after you and Graham were married. I knew my brother. When you kicked him out, he wouldn't have rested until he'd made a new one, cutting you off without a cent!"

"Cara—" LaDonna began.

"It's all right, LaDonna," Magda said. "I expected something like this. I know nothing about a new will, Cara. Not that I would have been too surprised if Graham had already made one, even though we were still legally married. I knew him, too, you see."

"You smug—"

Dunlap cleared his throat portentously. "I handled all your brother's legal affairs, Miss Thornton. This will was drawn by an attorney in Oklahoma City. Your brother brought it to me to be placed in his file two years ago when he moved to Buckskin. If he'd made a later will, I would have handled it. He did mention, some weeks back, that he was thinking about it, but he never got around to it. I imagine he was waiting until the divorce was an accomplished fact."

Get 2 books FREE
SEE BACK OF CARD FOR DETAILS

"But Magda gets everything!" Cara sputtered. "Graham didn't want that! If he knows anything, he must be fighting mad right now."

"What you or I think he might have wanted before he died or might be wanting at this moment, has no legal bearing on the situation," Dunlap said.

"It's a miscarriage of justice! She can't get everything! I'll sue! I'll—"

"Oh, Cara," LaDonna said unhappily.

Dunlap peered at the sputtering girl over his spectacles. "Before you become too agitated, perhaps you'd better hear what everything amounts to."

Whatever additional threat Cara had been about to make was forgotten as she caught the grave note in the lawyer's tone. Both LaDonna and Magda turned abruptly toward Dunlap, too. Magda's serenity appeared a bit ruffled. LaDonna's glance dropped to her clasped hands, as though she knew, or suspected, what Dunlap was going to say.

"In the last year or so, Mr. Thornton made a number of investments which were subsequently"—he cleared his throat—"revealed to be imprudent. I hasten to add that had I been consulted I would have strongly advised against every one of them."

Cara began to pace back and forth between the desk and the three chairs. "Must you always circle endlessly around the point before you get to it? What are you trying to say?"

Dunlap turned one thin hand over and looked at the neatly trimmed nails. "To put it in a nutshell, Miss Thornton, as of your brother's death, his assets, excluding the equity in the house where his wife is living and his half interest in Eagle's Nest Lodge, come to roughly seventy-five thousand dollars."

The blood drained from Magda's porcelain face, leaving only two spots of color on her rouged cheeks. So it was possible to unnerve her, after all, Mitch thought.

"That's impossible," Magda said weakly.

"It is quite possible to lose a fortune in commodity options virtually overnight, if one is foolish enough to risk it," said Dunlap disapprovingly.

"Seventy-five thousand!" A little bark of laughter exploded from Cara. She stopped in front of Magda's chair and planted her hands on her hips. "Hardly enough to keep you in the manner to which you've become accustomed, eh, Magda?"

Ignoring her, Magda turned to LaDonna, who was still studying her hands. "Did you know anything about this?"

"I didn't know—but I suspected he's lost a substantial amount of money. I had no idea it was this bad. Graham seemed anxious lately, but when I asked him what was wrong, he said he could handle it. I'm afraid Graham had taken over his father's role of trying to protect me from unpleasantness."

"Why didn't you tell somebody what was going on?" Magda demanded of Dunlap.

"Mr. Thornton was an adult in full possession of his faculties," said Dunlap defensively. "It was hardly my place to go behind his back and tattle to you or his mother."

"Graham became impatient with Oscar's conservative investment plan," LaDonna said, "but until his death Oscar continued to oversee the investments for all the family." She shrugged almost apologetically. "After all, it was Oscar who made the money, wasn't it? I can see now that he should have included Graham more in the decision making. As it was, Graham had had little experience before his father died. He had to take on all of it before he was prepared. I'm sorry, Magda."

Magda shielded her eyes with her hand. After a moment, she took her hand away and said, "I'll have to sell the house."

No one contradicted her.

"And I may have to come to work at the lodge, even though I'm sure I'll hate it. It seems I'm in no position to pick up and choose."

"We'll work out something," said LaDonna.

"Wait a minute," Cara blurted. "What about my trust fund? Graham was the trustee." She turned to Dunlap, her hands clenched.

"The news is quite a lot better there," said Dunlap, and Cara relaxed visibly. "As you know, I was co-trustee with Graham of your trust as well as your mother's. I continually reminded Graham that his father had always invested the trust funds conservatively and that he would expect us to follow his example. Graham didn't insist on putting your money into options, at any rate, though I disapproved of many of his stock choices. Most of them are traded over the counter. They pay no dividends and the price swings can be volatile. But I had to compromise on some of those. The stock portfolio is down about twenty percent since your father died."

Cara expelled a breath of relief. "I can live with that. Michael and I can go to Europe, as we'd planned. Isn't that right, Mr. Dunlap?"

Dunlap stared at her, unblinking.

"I can't believe Michael is willing to interrupt his medical-school training to follow you around Europe," LaDonna said with obvious exasperation. "Furthermore, I don't think this is the time to discuss it."

"Nor am I the person you should be asking," Dunlap said. "According to your father's instructions when the trust was established, if something happened to Graham, your mother, Magda and I were to become joint trustees. I have only one vote out of three now. Even if I were so irresponsible as to want to turn over the capital to you to spend as you please, I couldn't do it without the backing of at least one of the other trustees."

Cara leaned over the desk. "I absolutely refuse to accept Magda as a trustee!" she fumed. "I told you that on the phone the other day. Daddy didn't know she and Graham were going to get a divorce when he set up the trust."

Dunlap leaned back as though he feared she might hit him. "That's beside the point. The terms of the trust became irrevocable when your father died."

"We'll just see about that!" Cara snatched up her purse from the chair she had vacated and stormed across the office. "I'll find my own lawyer." She slammed out the door.

"I apologize for my daughter's rudeness," LaDonna said.

"Why should you apologize for her?" Magda snapped.

Dunlap stood up behind his desk. "I'll do everything I can to move the probate proceedings along."

Magda looked around the office as though waking up from a deep sleep in a strange place. As the two women prepared to leave, Mitch stood up, and both women glanced at him, perhaps startled to find him still there.

"Before you go, I'd like to talk to both of you."

"Do you want me to stay, Mrs. Thornton?" Dunlap asked, looking at LaDonna.

"Why, I don't know. I must get back to the lodge and pacify the Indians. The discovery of the Indian graveyard on lodge property has added fuel to an already tense situation. Two employees walked off their jobs without notice, and some of the other Indians are muttering about looking for other employment. I simply don't know how we'll manage if that happens."

"I suggested that Callie Roach call you about the Cherokee Historical Society taking over the graveyard site," Mitch said.

"She may have phoned the lodge and left word for me to call her." LaDonna looked less burdened suddenly. "If I turn that tract of ground over to the historical society, perhaps the Indians will be pacified."

Mitch doubted it, but he'd let LaDonna discover that for herself.

LaDonna wearily rubbed her temples. "Must we do this right now, Chief Bushyhead?"

"I'm afraid so. I need a statement from each of you concerning your activities last Monday."

Magda sat back down in her chair. She still appeared dazed. "Let's get it over with then."

"There's no need for you to stay, Mr. Dunlap," LaDonna said, sitting down, too.

The attorney left quietly. Mitch moved around the desk and took the chair Dunlap had been occupying. "I'd like to start with you, Mrs. Thornton," he said, directing the statement to Magda. "If you don't mind."

She waved a hand in a helpless gesture. "I mind like hell. I have my hands full, trying to figure out how I'm going to live. But I don't seem to have any other options at the moment. Go ahead."

"I'll be brief. Tell me, to the best of your recollection, about last Monday. Where were you all day? What did you do?"

"That's easy. I have a standing appointment at the beauty shop Monday mornings at eleven. Any of the operators can verify that."

"In Buckskin?"

"Yes, at the Hair Affair on Cedar. I usually get up in the morning about seven thirty or eight and I don't recall that Monday was any different. I didn't know it was the day on which my husband would be murdered."

Mitch looked at her impassively, not responding to the sarcasm.

She went on. "By the time I had breakfast, picked up around the house, showered, and dressed, it was ten thirty and I drove to the beauty shop."

"How long were you there?"

"It takes about an hour for a shampoo, set, and comb-out. I got a manicure while I was under the dryer."

Roo was writing rapidly, his pen moving across the page of his notebook. "Did you go directly back home?" Mitch asked.

She closed her eyes for a moment. She was still paler than normal, as though she were nauseous. She looked as if her insides had been scattered about by Dunlap's bombshell and hadn't quite settled back in their accustomed places yet.

"Let's see. I think—yes, that's right. I picked up some cleaning and a few groceries—at Wynn's IGA. I must have been back home by one thirty or two. I remember listening to the weather forecast as I was driving back. The forecaster said there would be several inches of snow in our part of the state before night. I'd given some thought earlier to driving to Tulsa to visit with friends. When I heard the forecast, I remember being glad I'd decided not to."

"What did you do when you got home?"

"I put away the cleaning and groceries. Then, I can't remember doing much of anything. After the snow started, I curled up in front of the fire with a book."

"Did you go to the lodge at any time last Monday?"

Her eyes narrowed. "No."

"Did you go anywhere, other than the places you've mentioned?"

"No."

"Did you talk to anyone after you returned home?"

"I don't think so—no."

"Excuse me, Magda," interrupted LaDonna. "Wasn't that the afternoon Freda Richards was collecting for the American Heart Association? Not long after the snow started. She came to my door while I was napping—around five, I think—and Cara gave her a contribution."

Magda looked at her blankly. "She missed me, I guess. She must have come by earlier, while I was in town."

Mitch made a mental note to check with Freda Richards. "Is there anything else you can remember about that day?" he asked Magda.

She shook her head. "It was a quiet, ordinary day."

Except for the fact that your husband was murdered, Mitch thought. He turned to LaDonna. "What else do you remember about last Monday other than Freda Richards's collecting for the heart association?"

"Well, Cara and I were at home alone all day until Michael came a little before eight. They left at eight to go to Tulsa, against my advice, as I believe I've told you already, and I was alone after that."

There hadn't been enough time for LaDonna to have gone to the lodge after Cara left and before Graham took his insulin injection, Mitch calculated. In fact, by eight probably a half hour or more had passed since Graham Thornton had injected the fatal dose of insulin. He was busy dying at about that time. Besides, LaDonna Thornton was apparently the only one close to Graham who gained nothing by his death.

"No servants in the house on Monday?"

"No. I only have a twice-weekly cleaning woman. She comes Tuesdays and Fridays."

"And you're sure Cara didn't leave the house anytime Monday before Michael came?"

"Quite sure. She slept until nearly noon. I remember wishing we could drive into Buckskin for lunch—anything to get out of the house for an hour or so. I'd been confined to it for several days. But I simply didn't feel strong enough to get dressed and go out, so I didn't suggest it. Cara made waffles and bacon for both of us, and we ate at about one. I napped for a couple of hours in the late afternoon, and I believed Cara did some hand laundry. The snow had started by the time I lay down, and there was no question of Cara leaving after that until Michael arrived."

But there had been ample opportunity for Cara to go to the lodge and return while her mother slept. Neither Cara nor Magda had an alibi that could be substantiated.

Mitch went back over the same ground again briefly with both women, hoping they'd remember something they hadn't mentioned before, but they held to their statements concerning their activities on the day of Graham Thornton's murder.

"I've been trying to get hold of Julian Moncrief," Mitch said. "Is he working today?"

"I don't know," LaDonna said. "I talked to my secretary on the telephone this morning, but I haven't been to the lodge yet today. My secretary said Julian was away all weekend. I expect he was interviewing for another job or jobs." She looked overburdened suddenly. "I suppose I'll have the problem of finding a new chef on top of trying to keep the Indians happy and running the lodge without Graham's help. Julian has made no secret of the fact that he wants to leave us. Would you like me to phone my secretary again and ask if Julian is there?"

"No, I'm planning to drive out anyway. There are still a few employees I want to talk to."

THIRTEEN

MITCH DROVE TO Eagle's Nest Lodge upon leaving the lawyer's office, while Roo returned to the station to type up the two women's statements. The police chief found Moncrief in his small office next to the kitchen. The chef was abrupt and impatient to be rid of Mitch, but he showed no concern when Mitch mentioned the rumor that Graham Thornton had lied about Moncrief, effectively preventing his getting a job at a Dallas hotel.

"It didn't require much detecting to learn that," Moncrief said shortly. "It's hardly a secret. Mr. Thornton would have resorted to any means to keep me here. But he wouldn't have succeeded. Once I've made up my mind, I can be very determined. I won't be intimidated by petty little tyrants like Graham Thornton."

"Then perhaps you'll tell me what you and Thornton argued about in his suite Monday evening."

The chef tried to appear unruffled, but Mitch noticed that he gripped the arm of his chair until his knuckles turned white. "Mr. Thornton and I disagreed on a number of occasions. I really can't recall if Monday evening was one of them."

"You were overheard telling Mr. Thornton not to push you."

He stared at Mitch for an instant, then tweaked his mustache agitatedly. "Oh, yes, now I recall. I went to Mr. Thornton's suite to inform him that I knew how he'd kept me from getting the Dallas job. I told him I intended to leave anyway, and there was nothing he could do to stop me."

"How did he react to that?"

His lip curled. "With his usual loud bluster. He said I'd have to have a favorable reference, and he'd see I didn't get one. He seemed perfectly confident that he could prevent my leaving by such underhanded tactics. As I've already said, he was wrong. The man was an egomaniac."

"So, when he said you wouldn't get a favorable reference from him, you told him not to push you?"

"Quite."

"I don't understand why Thornton wanted to keep you at the lodge if you were determined to go."

"My dear fellow, you have no idea how utterly impossible it is to lure a superior chef to a place like this. It's absolutely stultifying to one's creativity. The only reason I came was because my doctor recommended it, to cut down on stress. Alas, I discovered boredom can be as stressful as job-related pressures."

"How long were you in the suite?"

"Two or three minutes. Five at the most."

"Did Thornton leave you alone at any time?" Mitch asked the question, even though he knew Moncrief wouldn't admit to being left alone with the insulin. But he didn't think the insulin was tampered with while Thornton was in the suite. If Moncrief had done it, he'd gotten into the suite earlier in the afternoon.

"No," Moncrief said.

"What time did you leave the suite after you argued?"

"It couldn't have been much after seven. I know because I left my car at the lodge and walked home, arriving there at seven thirty-five."

"I tried to contact you several times Friday. I left a message on your machine."

"I intended to return your call later today. I didn't get back home until Sunday night."

"You were out of town all weekend?"

"That's correct. I flew to Houston Friday morning and on to Kansas City early Saturday. I interviewed for three head-chef positions, two at hotels, one at an exclusive country club. I have every confidence that I'll be offered at least one of them, perhaps all three."

"How long have you know that Graham Thornton was a diabetic?"

He shook falling dark hair out of his eyes, a faintly feminine gesture. "Virtually since the day I arrived at Eagle's Nest Lodge. Mr. Thornton liked to talk about it, for some reason. Perhaps it made him feel important or special in a bizarre sort of way. I don't pretend to know how his mind worked."

"Did Thornton take his insulin injection while you were in the suite?"

"No."

If Moncrief was telling the truth, Thornton must have injected the insulin before admitting the chef to the suite—between seven and seven fifteen. He had evidently intended to get something to eat at his mother's house.

Less than an hour after arguing with Moncrief, according to Joy Yeaky's statement, Thornton left the lodge. Perhaps he wandered through the snow, disoriented for a time before crawling into the Bronco. Or perhaps he became ill immediately after leaving the lodge and the Bronco was the closest shelter. He would have meant only to rest a while and regain his strength. According to the medical examiner, Thornton probably didn't know he was in a life-threatening situation until it was too late.

Mitch questioned the chef for another ten minutes but came up with nothing helpful to the investigation, except for the fact that Julian Moncrief argued with Thornton in Thornton's suite before Thornton left the lodge Monday night. Which he'd known already. He questioned a few other employees, whom he'd been unable to on Friday. No new information came to light.

FOURTEEN

MONDAY AFTERNOON, after Virgil's shift started at four, Mitch met with his three officers. That morning Duck had questioned Jack Derring, the lawyer Magda Thornton had hired to represent her in her divorce action.

"What did you find out from Derring, Duck?" Mitch asked when all four were seated in his office.

"Not a whole lot."

Mitch wondered if he'd made a mistake, sending Duck to question Derring instead of going himself. Probably not. Derring might have been even more closemouthed with Mitch.

"We already knew Thornton wanted to keep the divorce settlement as small as possible," Duck said. "When I mentioned that, Derring said sure, it's what Thornton would have liked, but he'd have given her half of everything before he'd have gone to court."

"Why did he draw the line at going to court?"

"Derring didn't tell me. Just said that Magda would have waited Thornton out, no matter how long it took. I guess it would've been worth waiting for."

"Unfortunately for her," Mitch said, "there was a drastic change in Thornton's net worth before he died." He summarized what had transpired Monday in Dewey Dunlap's office.

"Whew," said Virgil. "You've gotta be somewhat self-destructive to play commodity options. I always heard Thornton was worth a million, at least. I'll bet old Oscar Thornton didn't know his boy was a gambler at heart, or he'd have tied up his inheritance in a trust, like he did his wife's and daughter's.''

"The rumors of what Thornton was worth may have been exaggerated," Mitch said. "Those things usually are. Still, he lost a bundle."

Duck sat forward in his chair. "That must have thrown all the Thorntons into shock."

"Magda and Cara certainly," Mitch said. "La-Donna wasn't too surprised. She said she'd known Graham was in financial trouble. She just didn't know how bad it was."

"But Magda didn't know," Duck said. "I'll bet she knew there was no new will, though. She probably figured she didn't have much time before she'd be cut out. And I don't care what Derring says, they couldn't have been sure she'd get half of Thornton's assets—which they must have thought would amount to nearly a half million—in the divorce settlement. She killed the guy, I tell you."

"She sure figured to be comfortably well off if Thornton died while he was still her husband," Virgil agreed. "What do you think, Mitch?"

"Magda had the most to gain by Thornton's death," Mitch mused. "Rather, she *thought* she did. But I like Cara as a suspect, too. That girl's spoiled rotten. I gather as long as her father was alive, she got whatever she wanted when she wanted it. Graham Thornton threw a monkey wrench into Cara's money machine. She despised him, and I don't think she ever took no for an answer in her life."

"Probably never even heard the word until Oscar Thornton died," Roo put in.

Virgil shuffled the papers in the Thornton case file. "I don't think we can rule out Moncrief, either. He admits that he and Thornton had tangled before and that Thornton threatened to keep him from getting another job before he left the lodge Monday night."

On the face of it, Virgil had a point. But Mitch couldn't help thinking that Moncrief was too clever to have doctored Thornton's insulin, then gone back the same evening to confront him. If Moncrief knew the insulin had been tampered with, he wouldn't have needed to confront Thornton. All he would have had to do was wait for Thornton's next insulin injection to kill him. Unless he couldn't resist one last opportunity to tell Thornton what he thought of him.

"Do we know who had access to Thornton's suite?" Roo asked.

"They all did," Mitch said. "The family members and employees. LaDonna probably has a master key, which Cara would have had access to, and Graham could easily have left one in the house he shared with Magda. I called the lodge to make sure, a little bit ago. They keep a master key at the registration desk and another in the storeroom off the pantry. All the employees had easy access to one or the other. There are several other masters used by the housekeepers. None of the keys is missing, by the way."

"Whoever it was took a big chance, though," Virgil said. "They could easily have been seen going in and out of the suite."

"They must have known the comings and goings at the lodge well enough to pick a time when there was little chance of being seen," Mitch said.

"They could have used that outside door in Thornton's bedroom," Virgil said. "After the snow started,

I doubt anybody was wandering around outside to see them."

"Mitch, when are you going to talk to Larry Yeaky?" Roo asked. All three officers had read Mitch's reports in the case file, including the one detailing his interview with Joy Yeaky.

"In a day or two, if we don't turn up something before then." Mitch was still reluctant to interrogate Larry. He knew his attitude was unprofessional, but he couldn't visualize Joy as the killer and he disliked the idea of causing her any more trouble than she already had. Furthermore, he found it difficult to believe that Larry Yeaky could have gone to the lodge, gotten hold of a master key, entered and left Thornton's suite, and replaced the key where he found it, without being noticed by someone.

"Nobody's mentioned Nila Ridge," Roo said. "Have we marked her off the suspect list?"

"Nobody's been marked off," Mitch said.

"Nila's a good friend of Trudy's," Virgil said. "She's had more than her share of trouble lately. I sure hope she doesn't turn out to be the murderer."

Mitch hadn't realized Virgil knew Nila well. "Do you think she's capable of murder?"

"I guess almost anybody's capable, if you back him against the wall and keep him there."

Mitch remembered Nila's furtive exit from the public phone booth the previous Friday night and again was troubled by it. When he was at the lodge earlier that day, he'd seen her pushing a linen cart down a hall. Maybe he should have questioned her about the phone call then. But why would she admit anything incriminating? Still, he'd ask her about it the next time he was at the lodge, he decided. Perhaps tomorrow.

As the meeting was breaking up, Mitch sent Virgil to find out if Freda Richards had called at Magda Thornton's house to collect for the heart association on the day Thornton died, and if so, at what time.

Virgil hadn't returned to the station when Mitch left for the day, but he called Mitch later at home. Freda Richards had canvassed all the homes in Lakeview on the previous Monday. She couldn't say specifically what time she'd reached Magda's street, but she thought it was between two and three. No one had come to the door. Since Freda was so vague about the time, she might even have arrived at Magda's house earlier, before Magda got home.

Emily cooked dinner that evening and seemed to make more of an effort to converse with Mitch than she'd been doing of late. He presumed she'd been thinking about his relationship with Lisa Macpherson and was trying to come to terms with it. He didn't bring up the subject again, feeling that he should let Emily work it out at her own speed. He assumed she'd talk to him about it when she was ready.

He was tempted to call Lisa and tell her things were looking up. Later that night, he even went to the phone and started to dial Lisa's number. Before he finished dialing, he replaced the receiver. He was jumping the gun. It was probably going to take another day or two for Emily to come to grips with this thing. But she would, Mitch told himself. As Virgil had said, Emily was a sensible kid.

As it turned out, it took longer for Emily to come to terms with the situation than Mitch expected.

FIFTEEN

Tuesday, December 19

TUESDAY WAS EMILY'S last day of school before the Christmas holidays. She seemed preoccupied at breakfast, but Mitch was in a hurry to get to the station and didn't press her. Later, he realized that was a mistake.

After school, Emily and Temple stopped for a Coke in the coffee shop on Sequoyah. The day was clear, but it had turned colder, and they ran the last block, ducking their bare heads and clutching their coats rightly beneath their chins.

The warm, steamy interior of the coffee shop felt wonderful. Except for a handful of retired old codgers who spent their afternoons playing dominoes at a table in the corner, the coffee shop was deserted. The two girls took the booth farthest from the old men and a good distance from the door that admitted cold air along with other customers.

Liz Roberts often drove them home from school, but Temple's mother was in a club meeting that afternoon. Since the end of football season, Kevin Hartsbarger had chauffeured them a few times, but he'd left school early that day, after his last exam.

They still had several blocks to walk before reaching either of their houses, but they weren't thinking about that as they sipped their Cokes.

Temple slipped out of her blue wool coat. "Just think, two weeks without school. I feel as though I've been let out of jail, don't you?"

"I guess."

"Well, gee, don't be so happy about it."

Emily faked a big grin.

"How can you be so glum?" Temple asked. "We can stay up as late as we want and sleep in the next morning, for two whole weeks. And Sandra Dunne's party is tomorrow night. What are you going to wear?"

Emily shrugged. "I haven't thought about it."

"How about your red velvet skirt with my white silk blouse?"

"Do we have to talk about it now?"

Temple grabbed her straw and sipped loudly. "Ex-*cuuuse* me. I don't mean to bore you, Emily. Would you rather talk about geometry?"

That elicited a giggle. "I'm sorry to be such a downer. Thanks for offering your blouse. I may take you up on it—if I go to the party."

Temple stared at her in bewilderment. "What do you mean *if*? Everybody will be there."

"Kevin may not be able to go. His folks are talking about going to Wichita to see his grandparents tomorrow and staying overnight."

Temple made a face. "Parents can be a pain. It won't be the same without you. I'm taking Kevin's cousin. Did I tell you?"

"Only about a hundred times."

"You could go with us."

Emily stared at the steam-coated windows at the front of the coffee shop. "Maybe."

Temple decided they were getting nowhere with that topic. She'd been trying to cheer up her best friend all day, and she was growing a bit weary of Emily's lack of response. "Okay, let's make plans. What are we going to do this weekend? Mother said she might take us shopping in Tahlequah Friday."

"Actually, I'm thinking about going somewhere else for a few days."

"Where?"

"I don't know—just away, to be by myself." In the silence that followed, Emily made a slurping sound with her straw.

"That sounds almost like running away."

"Not really... well, maybe, sort of."

"You're kidding, right?"

"No."

Temple leaned over the table. "Because your father has been dating Mrs. Macpherson, you're cutting out? That's really crazy, Emily."

"You're entitled to your opinion," Emily said stiffly.

"Do you really expect him never to go out with another woman in his entire life?"

"It's not that. It's—he watches me all the time. I know he wants me to talk to him about her, and I don't want to until I'm good and ready. He's driving me insane."

"Running away won't help."

"I wasn't thinking of going very far or staying very long. I only want to be left alone for a day or two, so I can think."

"There's always the Starlight Motel," Temple said lightly, as though she didn't really believe Emily meant what she was saying.

"I wondered if maybe I could—well, stay at your house."

"Without telling your father? Forget it. My mother would call him first thing."

"Yeah," Emily muttered, "and he'd come and get me. He says I've already worn out my welcome."

"No, you haven't."

Emily propped her chin in her hand. "I don't suppose I could hide in your room."

"Get real! We'd talk to each other, we couldn't help it. And my folks would hear us. Besides, my mother breezes into my room whenever the whim strikes her. We've had big hairy arguments about it, so now she knocks and then she comes in. If I lock the door, she says if the house caught on fire, I might pass out from smoke inhalation before I could get out."

"I don't have enough money for a motel room. Daddy would find me there anyway."

"Emily, talk to him. Get it over with."

Emily set her jaw. "Not until I'm ready." A part of her knew that she wanted to punish her father with her silence, but she was too confused to feel guilty about it. She wondered what her mother would say if she knew Emily was thinking of running away. Nothing, of course. Her mother was dead. *Oh, Mother, why did you have to leave us?* "Never mind. I can always hitchhike to Tulsa. They have shelters for the homeless there."

"Homeless?" Temple giggled, but stopped abruptly when she saw Emily's furious glare.

Emily began buttoning her coat. "I'm glad you find this amusing, Temple."

"I don't," Temple said hastily. "I'm just knocked out by all of this. I don't know what to say."

"You could help me think of someplace to hide out for a couple of days." Emily sucked in her breath. "I just had a terrific idea. What about your folks' house in Lakeview, near the lodge?''

Temple's usual look of startlement was sharpened tenfold. "They'd kill us."

"Nobody but the two of us would ever have to know. I'll be home again before anybody misses me."

"But the lake house doesn't even have central heat. We don't go there in winter. There's only the fireplace and a portable electric heater for the bathroom. If you made a fire, somebody might see the smoke and call my folks."

"The electric heater would work. I could stay in one room and shut off the rest of the house. Get me the key, Temple."

Temple was already shaking her head. "We'd never get away with it. When my mother found out, she'd do something dreadful. Maybe take the door off my room. She threatened to do that once when I wouldn't open my door. I had my earphones on and couldn't hear her, but she didn't believe me. Plus, I'd be grounded until I'm thirty-five."

"She'll never know. Please, Temple."

"How—how would you get out there?" she sputtered. "You can't ask someone to drive you."

"I'll walk. It's not really that far."

"It's cold. You'll freeze."

"I'll dress warmly. Stop trying to talk me out of it, Temple. If I can't use the lake house, I'll—I'll take Daddy's tent and camp out in the woods."

Temple eyed her. She didn't really believe her, but what if she was wrong? What if they found Emily frozen stiff? It would be all her fault. She wasn't willing to take the chance. "Your dad will find you. He's the chief of police, for gosh sakes."

"He'll never think of looking in your lake house."

"I'm your best friend. He'll think of it."

"Well, I'll tell him I'm staying with you for a couple of days. I'll say I need to get away and think. You just have to make sure you answer the telephone if he calls. You can make some excuse, say I'll call him back later."

Temple sensed she was losing the argument. Emily was more determined than she. She leaned her head against the high back of the booth and closed her eyes. When she opened them, she said, "If you ever tell anyone I gave you the key, I'll kill you."

"I won't," Emily promised. "Besides, I'll have it back before your folks miss it." She slid out of the booth. "Come on. I need to pack a few things before Daddy gets home from work."

"I know I'm going to regret this," Temple groaned as she followed her friend out of the coffee shop.

WHEN MITCH GOT HOME that afternoon, the house had an empty feel. He found Emily's note on the kitchen table.

> *Dear Daddy,*
> *I'm going to stay with Temple for a couple of days. I have to get away so I can think. Please try to understand and don't make me talk about things until I'm ready. Please, Daddy.*
> *Love, Emily*

Mitch's first reaction was anger, and his first impulse was to phone the Roberts house and demand that Emily come home immediately. But he knew he shouldn't do anything until he'd cooled off.

He heated a can of chili for his dinner, fuming over this latest craziness of Emily's. Friends had told him about the rebellious teenage years, but he'd told himself Emily had no good reason to rebel. Apparently she didn't need a good reason.

By the time he sat down at the kitchen table with the chili and a box of crackers, he was thinking more rationally.

The atmosphere in the house had been as thick as cold molasses the past few days. Maybe he and Emily did need a little time apart, he as much as she. Emily would be fine with the Robertses. In fact, there was no place he'd rather she be as long as she didn't want to be home. He thought that Ellen would have said, "Respect her wishes. Wait for her to come to you." So he decided not to make the call.

SIXTEEN

Wednesday, December 20

MITCH WAS AWAKENED the next morning by the ringing of the telephone beside his bed. Dead to the world, he struggled to throw off the paralysis of sleep. He wondered groggily if Emily had changed her mind and wanted to come home immediately. He rolled over and reached blindly for the phone.

"Mitch Bushyhead speaking."

"This is Sophie Redeagle, Chief Bushyhead. I waited until I thought you'd be up. I hope I didn't wake you."

"No, it's fine. What can I do for you?"

"There may be nothing to worry about," she said hesitantly, sounding as though she wanted to convince herself.

"Did you call the police station?" From midnight to eight A.M., calls had been forwarded to Roo's house, since he was the officer on call that night.

"I didn't think anyone would be there. I'm sorry. I'm bothering you."

"It's no bother, Mrs. Redeagle. What is it?"

"I'm at my daughter's house. I spent the night with her children because she had to work late yesterday and—well, she didn't know how late she might be, and she said we should go on to bed when we were ready and not wait up for her. She didn't seem any more troubled than usual, you see. It never entered my mind she'd do something foolish."

"What has she done?"

"I don't rightly know. But when I got up this morning, I discovered she didn't come home at all last night. I checked where she works, and nobody's seen her since about six thirty yesterday. She works so hard, Chief Bushyhead, but she still can't make ends meet . . . and last Friday she got a bill, which there's no way on earth she can pay right now." The woman was speaking so rapidly that Mitch couldn't find a place to interrupt. "I can't give her any money. I only have my Social Security. I don't think she cares so much for herself, but my mobile home isn't big enough for the four of us, and she worries about moving her kids to some cramped little apartment. She loves those boys. That's why I can't believe she just up and ran off. Do you think that's what happened, Chief?" Her voice wobbled, and Mitch suspected she feared that's exactly what had happened.

"I doubt it. She's probably at a friend's house." He thought of the note Emily had left on the kitchen table. "Sometimes we need to get off by ourselves for a while. What's your daughter's name?"

"Nila Ridge."

ON THE WAY to the Ridge house, Mitch swung by the station to leave the Land Cruiser and pick up a patrol car and Duck, who'd just come on duty and was complaining mightily between swallows of coffee from a Styrofoam cup.

"My stomach's on fire," Duck whined. "I must've drunk five gallons of coffee last night. It's the only way I could keep from eating. Then I had to trot to the bathroom every twenty minutes. Couldn't sleep worth a hoot."

"Your stomach wouldn't bother you if you'd drink water instead," Mitch suggested. "Most people don't drink enough water. It's a known fact."

"You can drink ten buckets of water, and it still won't take the place of chicken-fried steak."

Mitch looked over at Duck approvingly. "Sounds like you finally got serious about your diet."

Grimacing, Duck set the half-full cup of coffee in the plastic holder attached to the patrol car's dash. "Geraldine did. She made me go see Doc Sullivan yesterday afternoon. Before supper."

"Good for Geraldine."

"Doc put me on a modified fasting program. You mix this powder with water. Five times a day. I got two doses in a thermos back at the station."

"You make it sound like medicine."

"That's what it seems like, only worse. Except for plain water, unsweetened tea, and black coffee, those little packets of powder are all I'm supposed to put in my stomach the first four weeks. After that, I get one meal a day—if you want to call it that. Baked fish and chicken and steamed vegetables."

"By then, it'll seem like a banquet. I'm proud of you, Duck."

He groaned. "You can tell the folks at my funeral. I don't think I'm going to live through the first week. Doc says, after that, something called ketosis sets in, which means you're not supposed to feel hungry anymore. I'll believe it when it happens. Provided I'm still among the living."

"Ketosis. Never heard of it."

"Maybe Doc made it up. How do I know?"

"I don't think he'd do that."

"Hmm. According to him, it's a kind of self-protective mechanism the body has."

"Ketosis?"

"That's what we're talking about, ain't it? Doc says it explains how people in a famine can starve to death without feeling hungry."

"Cheery thought."

"What I told Doc. He thought it was funny."

"Well, you won't starve. You've got that powder. If Doc's right, the hard part's the next six days. You can hold out that long."

Duck's stomach grumbled. He made a face and rubbed his belly as though comforting an old friend. "I dunno."

Mitch parked in the gravel driveway beside the Ridge house, an older home that had been spruced up with vinyl siding and storm windows before Nila's husband got itchy feet. The house was a neat, oblong box with hooks for an old-fashioned swing on the front porch. The big yard was surrounded by a chain-link fence. A comfortable home for the two Ridge boys to remember with nostalgia when they were adults.

Mitch and Duck crossed the yard, and Mitch rang the doorbell. Inside, they could hear Mrs. Redeagle telling Nila's boys to eat their breakfast.

"When's Mama coming home?" A young boy's voice.

"I don't know, Eugene. Go on, now. Your egg's getting cold."

The door opened. Sophie Redeagle's brown face was creased with lines of worry. She was short, like her daughter, but twenty pounds heavier than Nila. The anxiety in her black eyes eased a little as she took in the two officers. "I'm so glad you're here. Come in." She closed the door between the living room and kitchen.

She took the worn recliner at a right angle to the sofa where Mitch and Duck sat. Leaning toward them, she said in a low but tense voice, "I called the lodge again. Nila hasn't shown up for work, and she was supposed to be there twenty minutes ago. I hope she hasn't done something foolish. The statement she got was from the mortgage company. They said they'd foreclose on the house if she didn't pay what she owes them."

Mitch glanced at the telephone sitting on the table next to him and thought about Friday night. "Mrs. Redeagle, when did you last see Nila?"

She rubbed a spot in the center of her forehead, as though trying to relieve a sudden pain. "Yesterday morning. The boys were getting out of school for Christmas vacation yesterday, so I stayed all day and did some baking. Usually, I come at seven thirty, when Nila leaves for work, and stay with the boys until they go to school at eight forty-five. I come again after school and stay until she gets home. Yesterday she said she'd be very late."

"Because she'd be working."

"Well, she didn't say, but that's about the only reason she's ever late getting home."

"And she told you to put the boys to bed. Has she ever worked past the boys' bedtime before?"

Two parallel lines creased the spot in the middle of her forehead, and she rubbed it again. "No, now that I think about it. Usually if she works overtime, it's only for a couple of hours, till six thirty or seven."

"You didn't think it odd that she asked you to put the boys to bed and stay the night?"

"I did wonder. I didn't ask because—well, I could tell she didn't want to explain anything. Nila's like that, closemouthed, even when she was a child. And she's been even quieter than usual since she got that letter from the mortgage company Friday."

Friday, the night Mitch had seen Nila in town, using the pay phone. "What time did Nila get home last Friday?"

She looked distracted, and it took a few moments for her to answer. "I'm sure it was the usual time, around five. If she'd been late, I would remember."

"Did you go home then?"

"Yes."

So Nila had left the boys alone while she made her phone call. It had been that important to avoid risking their overhearing her conversation.

"Mrs. Redeagle," Mitch said, "I saw Nila leaving the public phone booth next to the post office Friday night. Have you any idea who she might have been calling from a pay phone?"

She was clearly bewildered. "No. Why would she leave the house to make a phone call, when she has a phone right here?"

"I wondered if she'd located her husband and didn't want the boys to hear the conversation."

"Richard? She hasn't heard a word from him, and she hasn't made any effort to find him. Trying to get child support out of him wouldn't be worth the effort. He's out of work more than not. It must have been someone else in the phone booth. It couldn't have been Nila."

"Maybe you're right, but I wonder if you'd ask the boys if she went out Friday night a little before eight. Just to be sure."

She rose and went into the kitchen. Mitch and Duck heard most of the conversation. Yes, both boys insisted, their mother did go out Friday night. She left them alone, saying there was something important she had to do. She wasn't gone long. They'd been watching a favorite television program when she left, and the program was ending when she returned.

Mrs. Redeagle came back into the living room. She looked quite worried. "You heard?"

Mitch told her there was probably a simple explanation, then said, "When you phoned me earlier, you told me you'd spoken to somebody at the lodge, who said Nila left work at six thirty yesterday. When did you make that phone call?"

"This morning as soon as I discovered Nila's bed hadn't been slept in. I talked to the woman who works nights at the front desk."

"Lucille Hummingbird?"

"Yes. She checked the time sheet and said Nila signed out at six thirty yesterday."

"Is there anywhere else she might have gone? A close friend? A relative?"

"Before I called you, I called everybody else I could think of. Nobody's seen her." She stared at her small brown hands for a moment. "I keep thinking about Mr. Thornton dying like he did and that Indian graveyard and what some of the Indians are saying." She looked up and smiled apologetically. "I've never put much stock in such as that, but it makes you wonder."

"Mrs. Redeagle, Graham Thornton wasn't killed by a witch." He had meant to reassure her, but she didn't appear relieved.

"No, I suppose not." Unhappily, she shook her head. "This has been building ever since Richard left.

That letter from the savings and loan was the last straw. She'll come back, once she'd thought it all through and figured out what she's going to do. She wouldn't desert her children, like Richard.'' She glanced hastily toward the closed kitchen door and added fiercely, ''I know my daughter.''

She didn't want to believe that Nila's disappearance might be related to Graham Thornton's death. Perhaps she couldn't bear the weight of such speculation. It was less frightening to believe her daughter had disappeared because of financial pressures she couldn't handle and would turn up in a few days.

Mitch requested Nila's car tag number, and Mrs. Redeagle left the room to search the desk in Nila's bedroom for the car's registration papers. Waiting, Mitch thoughtfully plucked a loose thread from the sofa's upholstered arm.

Duck's stomach grumbled and he sighed. ''My aunt did that once,'' he said.

''What?''

''Got fed up and disappeared for a few days. Left her five kids for her husband to worry about. She wrote him a note saying nobody appreciated her, and she wanted the old man to see how fast things would go to hell without her. Nila's old man beat her to it, though. I don't guess she'd want to prove anything to her mother, would she?''

''No.''

''You don't think she could've run off?''

''I wish I did.''

Mrs. Redeagle returned with the tag number, and Mitch and Duck rose to leave.

''You'll let me know the minute you find out something, won't you, Chief Bushyhead?''

"Yes, ma'am."

Back at the station, Mitch put out an APB on Nila's car. He left Helen in charge with instructions to call Virgil if an emergency arose. Then he drove to the lodge, followed by Duck and Roo in a second patrol car.

After questioning all the employees, they'd learned nothing new. One of the waiters had been crossing the lobby when Nila left the lodge at six thirty the previous evening, confirming the hour jotted on her time sheet. But the waiter had returned to the dining room without seeing Nila get into her car and drive away, which she'd obviously done since the car wasn't at the lodge.

In LaDonna Thornton's office, located on the opposite side of the lobby from Graham's, LaDonna was talking to Magda about menus. Magda did not appear to be enjoying the meeting, but evidently she felt obliged to take an active interest in the lodge, which represented the giant portion of the inheritance from her late husband.

LaDonna had given Mitch permission to use Graham's office for the interviews, where he and Duck talked to employees in batches of three or four while Roo took notes. Clearly LaDonna was not happy having them on the premises again. "All these questions are disrupting our work," she told Mitch before the interviews, with a severity he hadn't thought her capable of. She was clearly harried this morning.

"We'll interfere as little as possible," Mitch assured her.

"Well. Maybe it'll help you find Nila," LaDonna conceded. "I want to get all of this behind us. If we don't, the Indians are going to walk out of here en masse. They're already saying a Cherokee witch is responsible for Nila's disappearance as well as Graham's death.''

After the interviews, Mitch returned to LaDonna's office to thank her for her cooperation. Billy Choate was leaving as Mitch arrived. He gave Mitch a dark look and nodded without speaking.

Mitch tapped on the door. "Mrs. Thornton, it's Mitch Bushyhead."

"Come in," she called.

At a small table in one corner, Magda was now poring over a ledger and glanced up only briefly as Mitch entered. LaDonna was seated behind a walnut French provincial desk. She still seemed harried, Mitch noted, and dark smudges beneath her eyes indicated she hadn't slept well. Perhaps she was worried that she couldn't make a go of the lodge alone, even with Magda's help. The lines fanning out from her eyes seemed to have etched themselves deeper since Mitch had last seen her days ago.

"I wanted to thank you for accommodating us," Mitch said.

LaDonna waved a hand in acknowledgment. "Did you learn anything helpful?"

"Not really. I don't suppose Billy Choate told you anything new about Nila just now." Earlier, Billy had told Mitch that he'd seen Nila only once yesterday, before noon, and he hadn't talked to her.

"Him?" she said wearily. "He was here to issue an ultimatum. I've already turned over that Indian graveyard to the historical society. I thought that would satisfy the Indians. But now Billy says they want me to bring a Cherokee medicine man out here for some kind of mumbo jumbo."

"A medicine ceremony."

"Yes, that's what he called it. If I refuse, he says he'll quit and most of the other Indians will, too."

"Why refuse?"

"I'll be a laughingstock."

"Would you rather lose half your work force?"

"Do they actually believe there's some kind of evil witch at work here and that this medicine man can stop it? My God, in this day and age. It's absolutely barbaric."

"Maybe it seems barbaric because you don't understand it."

She lifted an eyebrow. "I'd forgotten. You're part Cherokee yourself. Have I insulted you?"

"No. But I can assure you the Indians are serious about this. They'll walk if you don't comply with their request."

She threw up her hands. "Our guests may look on it as local color. I'd better call Billy back and see if he can put me in touch with a Cherokee medicine man."

"I know one. He's called Crying Wolf. I'll talk to him about performing the medicine ceremony."

"I don't like this. It gives me the willies."

"I think it's fascinating," Magda said from the corner.

LaDonna glanced at her briefly. "Chief Bushyhead, do you think you can persuade this medicine man to come right away?"

"I'll tell him it's urgent."

"I'll pay his fee, of course, whatever it is."

"I'm not sure he charges a fee. I'll find out."

Mitch turned to Magda. "May I speak to you alone?"

She didn't look pleased, but she closed the ledger.

LaDonna rose. "I need to talk to the chef. Julian is leaving us at the end of January, and I want him to break in somebody new. I'll be back shortly, Magda." She closed the door behind her.

"Where is Moncrief going?"

Magda leaned back in her chair, her forearms resting on the table she was using as a desk. "A country club somewhere. Kansas City, I think."

"Did Mrs. Thornton give him a reference?"

"Of course. Julian's a snot, but he's an excellent chef."

Mitch made a mental note to check out Moncrief's background before he left town. The chef was low on his list of suspects, but still there.

"So you're going to be helping your mother-in-law run the lodge now," Mitch observed.

"Once I learn enough to be helpful. Right now I'm mostly in the way. LaDonna's trying to be a good sport about it, but she knows this is the last place I'd be if I had any other choice. My parents owned a motel. The whole family had to pitch in. I swore I'd *never* get involved in anything like it again. I made that clear to Graham when he and his father were building the lodge." Her full, red lips formed a self-deprecating smile. "Never is a long time, right?"

Mitch nodded.

"Sit down. Would you like a cup of coffee?" She seemed to have decided to make the best of a trying situation. An automatic-drip coffee maker sat on a small credenza. The glass carafe was half full.

"Sounds good," Mitch said. "Black, please." While she poured the coffee, he took out a pad and pen and settled in a chair. After handing him a cup, she returned to the chair behind her makeshift desk.

She watched him take a cautious sip. "Mr. Derring told me one of your officers was asking questions about my divorce."

"What else did Derring tell you?"

"That I don't have to give you the time of day if I don't want to."

The coffee was as weak as water. Mitch set the cup down. "He's right, but I can think of only one reason why you wouldn't want to cooperate in the investigation of your husband's murder."

"The reason being that I have something to hide?"

"Have you?"

"Chief Bushyhead, everyone is hiding something." She fingered a pearl earring. "But never mind that. We both have work to do. What do you want to know?"

"Why were you divorcing your husband?"

She gazed at him steadily for a long moment. "Incompatibility."

"Officially. And unofficially?"

Something shifted in her expression, an almost imperceptible distancing. Mitch sensed that she was hiding something, the same feeling he'd had when he and Sullivan had informed her of Thornton's death and she'd wanted to know who had killed him.

"He was a thoroughly detestable man."

"Yet you married him. Did he change so drastically after the wedding?"

With one finger, she traced the printing on the cover of the ledger. "I don't suppose he did. He merely stopped pretending to be someone he wasn't."

"Other women?"

"That, too." She appeared to be unruffled by the question.

"Anyone in particular?"

She dropped both hands out of sight behind the table. "No. I never blamed the women. Actually, I felt sorry for them. I knew they'd be disillusioned eventually."

"Did you ever confront him about the other women?"

She stirred restlessly. "In the beginning."

"What was his reaction?"

Something flickered in her brown eyes, something from deep inside her. It looked very much like pure rage. Then it was gone, and she was gazing at him coolly. "It was—unpleasant. Next question."

"Were you ever present when your husband and his sister argued?"

She visibly relaxed. "Several times. It was always over Cara wanting more money from her trust fund and Graham refusing."

"I take it Cara's father was more generous than Graham."

"When it came to Cara, yes," she said with an odd inflection. "Oscar doted on her. She had him wrapped around her finger. It was as if..." She paused to search for words. "Oh, as if Cara and Oscar were the family, and the rest of us were outsiders. That's the only way I can explain it."

"Didn't Mrs. Thornton and Graham resent that?"

"Graham certainly did. He disliked his father, but at the same time he was too much like him. Graham was always trying to prove himself to Oscar."

"And Mrs. Thornton?"

"LaDonna is LaDonna," she said with an enigmatic smile.

"Meaning?"

"The self-sacrificing type. Whatever Oscar wanted, Oscar got. She's from the old school. She made herself over to please him. Brought him his slippers. Laid out his clothes every morning. That kind of thing. When he died, she didn't even know who she was."

"She seems very competent to me."

"You're seeing the new LaDonna. After Oscar died, she began coming to the lodge and helping out. In the beginning, she was simply desperate to have something to do. It turned out she was good at it. Before that, I don't think she believed she was capable of accomplishing anything outside the four walls of her house. Now she's obsessed with the lodge, a workaholic. It's not that she has to work so hard. She likes it. Sometimes I look at her and I wonder where LaDonna the martyr went." She glanced at the ledger before her and her nostrils quivered, as though she found it as unsavory as a piece of rotting food. "I only wish I found working here half as absorbing as she does."

"If you hate it so much, you could sell your share."

"I've thought of it," she admitted. "But I want to give this my best shot first. And I don't know how easy it would be to find a buyer. There were some feelers recently, but they fell through. If I sell, I'd prefer to sell to LaDonna, and I don't think she could swing it now. She has enough on her plate. Besides having the full responsibility of the lodge, she's trying to deal with Cara, who keeps badgering her for money from her trust fund to go abroad."

"Will she give in to Cara?"

"Probably. Cara's relentless."

"You're a trustee now. Don't you have something to say about it?"

"I couldn't care less what Cara does with her money. Besides, if LaDonna agrees, she'll talk to Mr. Dunlap and he'll go along."

She raised both hands and lifted her heavy mass of red hair. "I'd just like to get out of this whole mess." She sounded quite grim. "I'll hold out as long as I can, for LaDonna's sake. But if I find I can't hack it, I'll put it to her straight. Buy me out or I'll find somebody who will." She dropped her hair and squirmed in her chair. "Look, it's been nice talking to you, Chief, but I really should get back to this."

Mitch thanked her and left.

BACK IN TOWN, Mitch stopped at Virgil's house. Virgil's oldest son, Donald, came to the door. "Hi, Chief. Come on in. Dad's in the kitchen."

The house was full of kids out of school for Christmas vacation. Virgil's six and two or three more, Mitch estimated on his way through the living room. The younger ones sprawled on the floor, watching television cartoons. The two older boys and another teenager sat around the coffee table, playing cards.

In the kitchen, Virgil was seated at the big oak table, reading the morning newspaper, oblivious to the noise from the next room.

"I need to make a call," Mitch said, and went to the kitchen wall phone. He dialed the Robertses' number. There was no answer. It was the second time he'd called to check on Emily and there'd been no one home. Liz and the girls were probably out shopping.

Mitch pulled out a chair. "You running a day-care center now?"

"I wish we *did* get paid for all the kids ours drag home. We'd be rich. We had two sleep-overs last night."

"Be glad they want to bring 'em home," Mitch advised.

Virgil folded the newspaper and got up to stack his breakfast dishes in the sink. "What's happening?"

"Nila Ridge has disappeared."

Virgil came back to the table and sank into his chair, stunned. "Say again?"

Mitch told him what he knew, concluding with, "Nobody's seen her since six thirty yesterday evening as far as we can find out."

"Good Lord."

"I put out an APB. If her car isn't spotted, we'll start asking questions in the area around the lodge this afternoon."

"Her mother could be right. She could be holed up somewhere for a few days. But you don't believe that, do you?"

"I have a real bad feeling about this, Virgil."

"Yeah. Me, too. Graham Thornton owned the lodge. Nila worked there. Has to be a connection." He drummed his fingers on the table. "Maybe Nila killed Thornton. If he'd lived, she was out of a job. When we started asking questions, she might have gotten worried that we were closing in on her. Stranger things have happened, but I can't really see Nila as a murderer."

"If she didn't kill him, she probably knew something about the murder that she didn't tell us."

"She could've been afraid to talk. Maybe she was warned off, threatened."

"Or she threatened somebody else." Mitch told him about Nila's call from the pay phone booth Friday night, after she'd received the letter from the mortgage company. "Desperation can make blackmailers of the most unlikely people."

"You're scaring me, Mitch. Nila's all those two boys have."

"They have a grandmother."

"When are you gonna start canvassing the neighborhood near the lodge?"

"Around two, I guess."

"I'll come to work early." A loud argument and the sound of scuffling broke out in the next room. Virgil raised his voice, "Hey, you broncs. Pipe down." To Mitch, he said, "Just what I needed. An excuse to get out of the house early. Trudy can't kick when duty calls."

"Is she around now?"

"In the basement, doing the laundry."

"I need to talk to Crying Wolf." Mitch explained LaDonna Thornton's dilemma. "I was hoping you'd come with me." Crying Wolf would be more likely to accommodate Virgil, a fellow Nighthawk.

"Sure," Virgil said eagerly. "Let me go tell Trudy."

THE OLD MEDICINE MAN lived in a cabin deep in the woods near Going Snake Mountain. Mitch hadn't been in the area since early in the fall, when an investigation had brought him there, and he'd have had trouble finding the turnoff if Virgil hadn't been with him. As on Mitch's previous visits, they had to leave the patrol car and walk the last several hundred yards. Thorny bushes and briars impeded their passage. Overhead, bare limbs created snaky patterns against the cold blue sky.

"The old man will die out here and won't be found for weeks," Mitch muttered, skirting a clump of dead blackberry vines. Crying Wolf was in his seventies.

"He wouldn't have it any other way," Virgil said. "He won't go to a hospital voluntarily. Death is natural. When it calls, you go to meet it alone and with dignity. That's the way he sees it."

The cabin sat in the center of a small clearing. The smell of burning cedar was strong, and smoke curled from the black stovepipe on the roof.

The door opened as Mitch and Virgil stepped on the porch. The old man's brown wrinkled face remained impassive as he looked at them, but there was a gleam of interest in his black eyes.

"We'd like to talk to you about a serious matter, Grandfather," Virgil said.

Crying Wolf looked from Virgil to Mitch and nodded. "You are welcome."

The interior of the two-room cabin was warmed by a cast iron wood stove. Two removable lids the size of dinner plates were recessed in the top of the stove. They were lifted by fitting the sharp end of an iron handle into matching indentations in the lids, for feeding the fire. The aroma of cedar was quite strong but not unpleasant.

The first time Mitch had visited the cabin, he'd sat on the faded linoleum-covered floor with the old man. Today Crying Wolf invited them to take two straight-back wood chairs near the stove. He sat on a low bench facing them. Linoleum was cold in winter.

Crying Wolf's gray hair along with pieces of bright-colored yarn was plaited in two braids that hung down his back. He wore overalls with a faded flannel shirt. Insulated underwear showed at the open collar.

Mitch explained what they wanted, and the old man listened with intense concentration.

When Mitch finished, Crying Wolf got up to add a log from the pile behind the stove to the fire. He stared into the flames for a moment before replacing the lid. "I have heard of the white man's death," he said. He sat down. "What you have told me of Nila Ridge worries me deeply."

"The employees at the lodge are worried, too," Mitch said. "They're going to quit unless a medicine ceremony is performed."

"Do you feel up to doing it?" Virgil asked.

Crying Wolf's black eyes studied both men gravely. "It is not how I feel that matters. *Sv:no:yi* must be trapped and killed before their evil will end."

"How soon can you do it?" Mitch asked.

The old man's thoughts turned inward, and he did not reply for several moments. He seemed to have forgotten they were there. He was the most serene person Mitch had ever met.

Crying Wolf's eyes focused slowly on Mitch, as though he was coming out of a trance, and he seemed to shiver. Mitch had the eerie feeling that he was preparing himself to do battle with powerful forces that would drain the old man's strength from him. It was not a mission he would have chosen, and he dreaded it.

"It will require three ceremonies—at daybreak, midday, and near dark. Tomorrow I will be ready."

"I'll come and get you at five A.M. It takes about thirty minutes to drive to the lodge. Will that give you enough time?"

Crying Wolf nodded. "I will need a tent."

"Sir, I'm sure Mrs. Thornton will provide you with a room at the lodge."

"You do not understand." He sounded disappointed in Mitch. "This night walker is very powerful. He must see that I am not afraid to set up my tent on the ground where he works his evil. I cannot hide in a white woman's house."

"I have a good, tight tent," Virgil offered.

"I will also need firewood."

"I'll see that you have plenty of wood," Mitch said.

"Then I will be ready to go with you at five tomorrow morning. Do not be late. I must be there when dawn breaks."

SEVENTEEN

Thursday, December 21

CRYING WOLF sat in the opening of the tent, staring into the flames that licked around the logs. With the going down of the sun, the evening had grown frigid. Fingers of cold were worming their way through the blankets he had wrapped around him. A part of his mind could feel them. The other part of his mind was seeing pictures in the orange flames.

There was a figure, writhing. He felt the pain in his own body. There a wolf's face, mouth drawn back from razor-sharp teeth. There a hand. He felt the gush of blood when it was severed from the body.

He had seen many fire pictures during the hours he'd sat motionless in the tent, most of them so terrible that he felt weighed down with the horror they depicted.

There was evil in this place. He had felt it the instant he got out of Mitchell Bushyhead's car, which the police chief had driven around behind the lodge and stopped at the edge of the woods concealing the Indian cemetery.

At first, Crying Wolf had helped the police chief unload the wood from the back of the vehicle. Bushyhead had said he'd bought it in town. The white woman who owned the lodge had paid for it.

After a few minutes, Bushyhead had told him to rest and let him finish unloading the wood. Then he'd set up the tent and helped Crying Wolf start a fire. It was still dark when Bushyhead drove away.

As the sky began to turn from black to gray, Crying Wolf had walked to the rim of the lake. Taking the pouch of unadulterated *tso:lagayv:li* from his coat pocket, he had mixed a small portion with Cotton Bowl twist and remade it, infused it with magic, with the proper incantation chanted in Cherokee.

The tobacco remaining in the pouch was the last of his carefully doled out supply of *tso:lagayv:li*, the most powerful tobacco that could be used in a medicine ceremony. It was grown under stringent restrictions and therefore was not easy to come by. But he had known he must call on all the power at his command for this day's work.

He had repeated the ceremony on the shore of the lake at noon and at dusk. Frequently, he heard cars coming and going and sometimes he had been aware of curious white faces watching him from the windows of the lodge. Those people had no notion of the danger they exposed themselves to by being in this place. They didn't sense the evil as he did.

Yet he knew the feeling would grow much stronger at full dark. The night walker slept during the day, drawing strength for the dark hours. Crying Wolf murmured to himself in Cherokee, gathering his own strength.

He could feel the night walker stirring now, waking up. It was time.

He rose to his knees, letting the blankets fall to the ground. He took the cigarette containing the *tso:lagayv:li* out of his coat pocket. Bending down, he touched the tip of the cigarette to an ember that glowed in the ashes near the fire.

He drew in the powerful smoke, rose, and swayed for a moment, light-headed from lack of food. He had fasted all day. When his head stopped spinning, he walked in a wide circle that enclosed the white woman's lodge and its grounds. He blew smoke as he walked, measuring it out slowly to make the cigarette last until he had completed the circle.

Finally he was back where he'd started. When the night walker, in whatever guise, tried to cross the smoke line, he would die.

Crying Wolf felt as weak as a kitten who didn't have its eyes open yet. Abruptly, he sat down on the ground. Fighting the night walker had taken all his strength. He was old. He did not know how much longer he would be able to come when he was called on to help his people. He took comfort from the knowledge that there were younger men who could take his place.

Some time later—Crying Wolf did not know how long—he heard Mitchell Bushyhead's voice.

"Are you all right, sir?"

Crying Wolf answered automatically in Cherokee, then remembered that the police chief could not understand his father's tongue. "I am weary," he said.

"Are you finished here?"

"Yes."

Then Bushyhead was helping him up, guiding him to the car. "I'll get the tent and put out the fire."

Crying Wolf put his head back against the car seat and slept.

LUCILLE HUMMINGBIRD put her three children to bed before she talked to her husband about the thing that had plagued her mind all afternoon and evening. It was ten after nine, and she had to leave for her night job at the lodge in half an hour.

Ever since she had heard of Nila Ridge's disappearance, she had been thinking about the night of the snowstorm, the night Graham Thornton had died. Something about that night kept nagging at her, but she hadn't been able to pin it down until today, when she'd seen the van in town, seen who was driving it.

She'd been headed for the supermarket. As she'd pushed the grocery cart around the store, telling Davy and Carol Ann to stay close and help her keep an eye on Jill, she'd relived that treacherous drive again. Snow driving into the steamy windshield. Wiping away condensation with her glove. Searching for a landmark that would tell her the truck was still in the right lane. Hazy headlights approaching too fast. She had thought at the time that it looked like a van. The warning blare of the driver's horn. Then fighting the steering wheel to make the turnoff as the oncoming van sped past. From the corner of her eye, she had caught a flash of color, the side of the van. She knew then what she'd been trying to remember.

In the living room, Henry was sitting on the edge of his chair, watching a boxing match on TV. Lucille had never understood why men liked such violent sports. As far as she was concerned, calling it a sport was merely a way to let men hurt each other with impunity.

She got her coat from the hall closet and dropped it on the sofa. "Henry, I need to talk to you before I go to work."

"What?" His eyes didn't leave the screen.

"I said I need to talk to you."

He glanced at her distractedly, then focused on the screen again, where one man had his opponent against the ropes and was pounding him unmercifully. "What about?"

He flinched as the boxer against the ropes took a blow to the midsection. "How is that guy still standing?"

"Henry—"

"Wait'll this round ends."

Sure. If the house was on fire, she'd have to wait for the end of a round to get it through Henry's head. She sat on the sofa, holding on to her temper. There were worse flaws in a man than being addicted to television prizefights. Some husbands spend their evenings in bars.

She had waited all day. Another minute wouldn't matter.

When the round ended, Henry turned to her. "Now. What were you saying?"

"The sound."

He picked up the remote control and turned it down.

"You remember the night Mr. Thornton died?"

"When it snowed so hard, yeah."

"I recalled something today." She told him what had been plaguing her. "Do you think it's important?"

"How would I know? Talk to Chief Bushyhead."

"What if I'm wrong—or there's no connection?"

"Let the police sort it out." His gaze was already straying to the television screen.

She had known all along what she ought to do. She'd just wanted Henry to say it. The problem was she could be harming two innocent people. Joy Yeaky had been on edge since the murder. Lucille knew Joy was spending her mornings looking for another job. She didn't think she'd found one yet, or Lucille would have heard.

But now Nila Ridge was missing. Lucille was sure Nila wouldn't leave her boys, even for a few days, without letting her mother know where she was going. She wouldn't walk out on her job, either. Wherever Nila was, she hadn't known she was going, and she hadn't gone there by choice.

Lucille put on her coat and gloves. She dropped a kiss on the top of Henry's head. "See you in the morning."

He managed to tear himself away from the boxing match long enough to say good-bye and kiss her properly.

EIGHTEEN

Friday, December 22

THE HOUSE-TO-HOUSE canvas in the residential addition of Lakeview the previous afternoon had turned up
no one who had seen a car matching the description of
Nila Ridge's. The next morning, Mitch sent Duck and
Roo back to finish the job. It would probably take all
day.

Mitch called the Robertses' house and Temple answered. Mitch identified himself and asked, "How are
things over there?"

"Fine. Great."

"Tell Emily I'll be there this evening to take her
home."

"Uh—okay. I gotta go now, Chief Bushyhead."

As soon as Mitch hung up, Bob Devay, the mayor,
called, wanting to find out what was happening in the
Thornton case. Mitch inferred that he was expecting a
break any day.

"Buckskin is becoming the murder capital of north-
eastern Oklahoma." Devay exaggerated a lot. "Graham Thornton makes three this year." He sounded as
though Mitch was somehow to blame. Mitch could always bank on the mayor irritating him in the first three
minutes of their conversations. Apparently the mayor
hadn't heard about Nila Ridge's disappearance yet.
Mitch didn't enlighten him.

"We wouldn't be spread so thin if the council would cough up the money for another officer."

"We talked about that at last week's council meeting, Mitch. We're trying to figure out where the money's coming from."

Mitch knew for a fact that the city had nearly fifty thousand dollars drawing interest in a money market account. When he'd brought that up at a council meeting, Devay had said the money was earmarked for street improvements.

"We could probably pass another penny of sales tax, if the council got behind it the way they lined up with Oscar Thornton on the annexation."

"We want to explore every other avenue first, Mitch."

The council members feared they'd be voted out at the next election if they backed the tax. Mitch had never understood why they wanted to be councilmen in the first place. They received no pay, and somebody was always calling them to complain about something. Made them feel important, Mitch guessed. He turned away from the window and saw Lucille Hummingbird hovering in his office doorway. "Gotta go, Devay."

"Chief Bushyhead?"

"Hi, Lucille. Come on in."

"You sure I'm not disturbing you?"

"Not at all." He ushered her to a chair, then returned to the creaking swivel chair behind his desk. "What can I do for you?"

"Something's been bothering me, about the night Mr. Thornton died. I couldn't think of what it was until yesterday. It's probably nothing, but Henry said I should talk to you."

Mitch felt a little prickle at the base of his skull. Perhaps this was the lead he so desperately needed. He got up to close the office door. "I'm glad you came in, Lucille."

"I was driving to work. It was snowing hard. You remember that night."

Mitch nodded encouragingly.

"I couldn't even tell if I was on the road or off it. So I wasn't paying that much attention to anything but driving. Henry said I shouldn't even go to work that night."

She was obviously reluctant to get to the point. "Go on."

She shifted uneasily. "I don't want to cause trouble for anybody. I don't think it's important anyway. It was between nine thirty and ten, and I heard Mr. Thornton died long before that, from the injection he gave himself before he left the lodge."

Mitch stifled his impatience. "Sometimes it's a trivial little detail that helps us solve a case. If it's not important, there'll be no harm done."

"You're right. It's just that Joy has been so upset lately and—"

"Joy Yeaky?"

"Yes. There was this van, you see. It passed me on the highway as I was turning off for the lodge. It was going so fast, I don't know how he kept from losing control."

"He?"

She sighed. "Larry Yeaky. I think it was his van. As it passed, I noticed that the side was two colors. Yellow and blue. I didn't think any more about it until I saw Larry Yeaky driving his old van in town yesterday. The back part of it is blue, and the front is yellow. I guess he started painting it and lost interest before he finished.''

"You say he passed you on the highway? He didn't come out of the road leading to the lodge?''

"I'm sure of that," she said emphatically. "I saw his lights before I reached the turnoff...only, well, there's the service entrance, about a half mile farther out than the main road. I didn't see him come out of there, you understand. But the way he was driving, like something wild, and with''—she looked away from Mitch quickly, and he knew she was thinking about Thornton's affair with Joy Yeaky—"everything else, I thought you should know."

Neither of the Yeakys was at home when Mitch reached their house fifteen minutes after Lucille Hummingbird left his office. Maybe the trade school in Tahlequah didn't give their students the generous holidays provided by the public schools. Or maybe Larry had gone with Joy, job hunting.

The van was in the garage, but the Bronco was missing. Mitch drove around town but didn't spot the Bronco. He'd ask Helen to keep phoning the Yeaky residence until she found somebody at home.

Mitch told himself not to expect Lucille's tip to lead anywhere. Thornton had been dead for at least an hour before Lucille saw Yeaky's van. And Larry would have had to gain entrance to the suite sometime before that. Joy had access to a key, and it was conceivable Larry could have gotten his hands on it, had a copy made, and returned it with no one the wiser. But that would mean that Larry knew about the affair and had laid his plans carefully over several days.

Furthermore, if Larry was the culprit, it didn't make sense for him to hang around the lodge for two or three hours after being in the suite before heading back to town. But what *had* he been doing out there on a night like that? Where could he have been coming from if not the lodge?

EMILY WISHED KEVIN and Temple would show up. Temple had promised to call Kevin this morning and ask him to drive her out to the lake house to pick up Emily and take her home. But it was after noon and there was still no sign of them.

Maybe Temple hadn't been able to get hold of Kevin. Maybe he hadn't returned from Wichita yesterday, as he'd expected to. Or maybe Temple's mother had forced Temple to go somewhere with her. Hadn't Temple said something about doing last-minute Christmas shopping today? It would be just like Mrs. Roberts to haul Temple off, even if Temple didn't want to go. They might not get back until after dark.

Emily had been at the lake house for three nights and two full days, afraid to open the blinds. Somebody might notice the change and call the Robertses to report it. Now the third day was half gone, and she was beginning to feel claustrophobic. To tell the truth, she'd have gone home yesterday if she'd had a ride.

She sighed and wrapped the quilt more tightly around her. Even though she had closed off the living room and had placed the electric heater near the couch, she still felt chilled. She'd had to pile four blankets on top of the quilt last night before she could sleep. The blankets were now folded and returned to the linen closet, where she'd found them.

Fortunately she hadn't had to walk to the lake house from town, carrying a change of clothes and the food she'd picked up at a convenience store. When she left the store, she ran into a boy who was in her history class. He lived out on Highway 10, past the lodge, and she'd hitched a ride with him. She'd told him she was going to house-sit for a family for a couple of days and had asked him to drop her at the stone-pillared entrance to Lakeview. It was dark by then, and she didn't think anyone had noticed her entering the house.

So how had her father discovered she was missing? Had he phoned the Robertses and talked to one of Temple's parents before Temple could answer? Something like that had happened because Officer Duckworth and Officer Stephens had knocked at the door about eleven that morning. What reason could they have for coming there, if they weren't looking for her? Yet when no one answered the door, they'd returned to the squad car and driven away. She couldn't understand why they'd given up so easily if they knew where she was. And it seemed odd that her father had sent them, instead of coming himself. Odder still, she'd seen the two officers driving down the street again an hour later.

The only explanation she could think of was that her father had discovered she was missing but not where she was. Maybe the policemen had gone house to house in town before coming out to search the Lakeview addition. If so, everybody in Buckskin would know she'd disappeared. She'd be bombarded with questions when school started again. How embarrassing! As bad as that would be, she was more worried about her father's reaction. She wanted to get back home before he found her. She'd begun to feel that this whole thing was getting out of hand.

Coming to the lake house had been a stupid idea in the first place. She could have thought things through just as well in her room. It had seemed kind of romantic and daring at the time, like a poor artist leaving civilization behind to go to a desert island and paint. She had read a book once in which that had happened. She wouldn't make a good artist, she thought. She'd been isolated in the lake house for less than three days, and she was already bored to distraction.

Her anger at her father had about fizzled out, too. Once she'd made herself imagine her mother alive and her father dead, she was no longer so certain her mother would have remained a widow, mourning her father, for the rest of her life. Her mother had had lots of friends, and before she got sick she'd been excited about finishing her college-degree requirements and teaching in elementary school.

Emily's mental picture of her mother confined to the house if her father had died, preserving it as it had been, like a shrine, didn't hold up on reflection. She would have mourned, but then she'd have gotten on with her life. As much as Emily hated to admit it, she might even have fallen in love with another man. She might have married him. Emily's father was almost forty, which sounded old to her, but she guessed it wasn't old enough to want to be alone for the rest of your life.

Besides, Emily thought, she couldn't stay outraged forever. That was juvenile. In fact, she'd acted pretty childish about the whole thing. She'd always been irritated by friends who pouted when they were mad at her. But that's what she had been doing. Even Kevin thought she was being unreasonable. She sighed. Kevin was probably right.

She heard a car and rose from the couch eagerly, but the car didn't stop at the lake house. Holding the quilt around her, she wandered around the room. What was keeping Kevin and Temple?

She bent and reached for the book she'd found in the bedroom but tossed it aside again unopened. She wandered to a side window and peeked through two slats in the venetian blinds.

The houses in Lakeview sat on large lots and were situated for maximum privacy. Only one house was visible from the living room. She'd heard cars coming and going a few times, but the garage was behind the house and the driveway led to a side street on the opposite side of the house.

Emily had seen only one person around the house next door since she'd arrived at the lake house. The first evening she was there, she happened to be looking out the window when a car stopped in front of the neighboring house. A woman got out, started across the yard, then turned around and returned to her car. Emily thought she was leaving, but she'd watch her drive around the corner and turn back toward the house, following the driveway that Emily couldn't see. A moment later, she'd heard a car door slam. The woman had entered the house by the back door, which was also out of Emily's line of vision.

She had wondered what the woman was doing there. It was dark, but when the woman had left her car and started toward the house, her face had been illuminated briefly by the yard light near the front door. It was Nila Ridge, and Emily knew that Mrs. Ridge lived in town.

Emily had entertained herself for a while, fabricating reasons for Mrs. Ridge being in the house next door. She was having a passionate love affair with the resident of the house, whoever that might be. Emily had heard that Mrs. Ridge's husband had left her, and maybe she'd already found a replacement.

Perhaps Mrs. Ridge was part of a secret society that met next door. A coven of witches, maybe. But Emily had to abandon that scenario almost immediately. She hadn't heard any other cars arriving.

Mrs. Ridge had probably come to visit a friend who lived next door. That wasn't nearly as intriguing as the other stories Emily's imagination came up with, but she had to admit it was the most reasonable explanation. They must have had a lot to talk about, too, because Emily didn't hear another sound from next door until after midnight, when a revving engine woke her, as though Mrs. Ridge were racing the engine for a minute to warm it up before she drove away. Didn't she know that's hard on the engine, she'd wondered, irritated at being roused from sleep.

It had been a while before Emily could fall asleep again. She'd lain beneath the pile of blankets on the couch, staring into the darkness. She couldn't turn on a light and read, for fear it would be seen by somebody driving down the street. Even though it was very late, she couldn't take the chance.

Nothing was going on next door now. She released the venetian blind. Where on earth were Kevin and Temple? There was no telephone at the lake house. She wished she'd thought about how isolated she'd be out here.

It would start getting dark before six o'clock. She'd wait until four, she decided. If Kevin and Temple weren't here by then, as cold as it was, she'd start walking.

NINETEEN

HELEN CALLED THE YEAKY house at intervals all day, but the phone was never answered. At four, when Virgil came on duty, Mitch decided to make another pass through town, looking for Larry.

Fifteen minutes later, he was driving slowly along Highway 10, approaching the Three Squares Cafe. Braking suddenly, he whipped into the parking lot. At this time of day, between coffee breaks and dinner time, only two other vehicles were parked at the Three Squares. One of them was an old blue-and-yellow van, the one he'd seen in the Yeaky garage earlier.

On one side of the café, an elderly man was eating a piece of pie. On the other, Larry Yeaky sat alone in a booth, a cup of coffee in front of him. He was leaning forward, his forearms braced on the table, his head down. He seemed to be staring into his coffee cup. Mitch had the feeling he'd been sitting like that for some time.

Mitch hung his jacket on the rack near the door. Larry looked up abruptly as Mitch slid into the booth across from him. an instant passed before he seemed to take Mitch in. His mind had been far away. "Hi, Chief." Then his gray eyes were wary. He was a good-looking young man, big and strong. Right now, though, the whites of his eyes were webbed with spidery red lines and he needed a shave.

"You're a hard man to run down, Larry. I've been looking for you all day."

He hesitated before he said; "I took Joy to Tahlequah to apply for a job. We had lunch and drove
around. We'll probably move there if she finds something."

"When did you get home?"

Fully alert now, Larry frowned. "Barely in time for
Joy to let me out at the house and get to the lodge by
two. Why have you been looking for me?"

"I need to talk to you."

"What about?"

Dicey Morgan, one of the evening-shift waitresses,
came out of the kitchen through the swinging door.
"What'll you have, Chief?"

"Nothing." Mitch didn't take his eyes off Larry.

"The cook made peach cobbler this morning."

"Nothing, Dicey," Mitch repeated.

The waitress shrugged and went back through the
swinging door.

"Where were you between seven and ten the night
Graham Thornton died?"

Larry darted a glance at the door, as though he'd like
to make a run for it, but he thought better of it. "At
home, I guess. I'm usually at home evenings since Joy
started working that shift. Why do you want to
know?"

Mitch ignored the question. "Think, Larry. It was
the night of the snowstorm. You should remember if
you were out in that."

He was already shaking his head. "I was at home.
The van's tires are pretty worn, and Joy takes the
Bronco to work. I wouldn't have risked driving the van
that night."

Mitch held his gaze until Larry looked down. Larry
picked up his cup, swallowed, set it down. He gripped

his spoon, then seemed to realize his nervousness was showing and dropped it as though it were hot.

"The truth is going to come out eventually, Larry," Mitch said. "Why don't you level with me?"

"I have," he insisted, not very convincingly. "Why would I lie about something like that?"

"Your van was seen coming from the lodge between nine thirty and ten that night."

Larry sucked in a breath, as though he'd received a physical blow to the midsection. Yet he seemed to have been expecting some kind of blow. He slumped back in the corner formed by the wall and the back of the vinyl booth. "I remember now. I did drive out that way the night of the snowstorm, but nobody could have seen me coming from the lodge because I didn't go there."

"Where did you go?"

Mitch could almost see the gears turning as he searched for a reasonable answer, but there was nothing beyond the lodge for several miles.

"Okay." His whole body seemed to sag. "I started to the lodge, but I changed my mind."

"Why? You must have thought it important to go out there originally, or you wouldn't have been driving that night."

He was mute, staring at his hands.

"You had something to settle with your wife, didn't you? Something that couldn't wait until she got home."

Without looking up, he muttered, "You know about Joy and Thornton, don't you?"

Dicey started to the table with the coffeepot. Mitch waved her back impatiently. "I've heard about the affair from several sources. How long have you known?"

He drew a ragged breath. He still wouldn't look at Mitch. "I heard about it that day."

"The day of the storm?"

"Yeah. The guy who rides with me to Tahlequah told me on the way home. I almost punched him out. I didn't believe it at first. I told him if he repeated what he'd told me to anybody else, I *would* beat the crap out of him. He said it was all over town anyway."

"And?"

Another deep breath. "I took him home and went home myself."

Mitch waited, but Larry said nothing more. Apparently Mitch would have to drag it out of him. "What happened then?"

"I couldn't stop thinking about it."

"That's the sort of thing a man doesn't forget easily."

He nodded. "I remembered how jumpy and irritable Joy had been lately. It's not like her. Some nights she couldn't sleep. I'd wake up and hear her moving around the house at all hours." He rubbed a weary hand over the stubble on his face. "Every time I asked her what was bothering her, she'd say nothing... nothing." He made a sound in his throat, as though the words were choking him.

"And you decided it might be true, after all."

"I didn't know, but the thought of it made me madder and madder. Finally, I thought if I could see them together, I'd know for sure. I was planning to get to the lodge before Joy left and, if Thornton wasn't around, make her go to his suite with me. I had to know, one way or the other." He looked at Mitch beseechingly then, as though begging him to understand.

"What made you change your mind?"

"I wasn't thinking very straight. I was driving too fast. I barely missed going off the road twice. I was afraid I'd lose control of myself when I saw Joy, I was so mad. So I went past the turnoff and drove until I found a place to turn around. I wanted to get back home before Joy did. I thought by then I could talk to her without losing my temper. The phone was ringing when I walked in the house. It was Joy. She said Thornton was dead, and she had to wait there until the police came. She was really shook."

"You never told her you knew?"

He shook his head. "When she got home she was a wreck. She started crying the minute she saw me, and I thought she wasn't going to stop. She's still not sleeping very well. I'm really worried about her, Chief."

Larry's story had the ring of truth. Once he'd realized he couldn't lie his way out of it, he hadn't faltered in his description of what had happened that night. He was hot-tempered. He could easily have behaved exactly as he'd said.

Larry looked at Mitch now and said earnestly, "I've been thinking about it a lot." When he should be sleeping and shaving, Mitch thought. "I know Joy loves me. If she was getting it on with Thornton, he forced her—somehow."

Mitch could see he desperately wanted to believe it. "Maybe the first time, but after that, why would she stay there and take it again. Why wouldn't she report it?"

Confusion flitted across his face. "I don't know. I didn't know Thornton. Maybe he was some kind of pervert. Maybe he threatened to hurt her real bad if she told. Kill her, even." All at once his eyes misted over.

He rubbed at them angrily. "A couple of times I saw bruises on her arms like somebody had grabbed her hard."

"Didn't you ask her about it?"

"Sure, and she said she must've run into something, like it wasn't important. Now I think he hurt her, and she was afraid to tell me."

Joy Yeaky had misjudged her husband. He was dying inside, yet he'd said nothing to her. He was protecting her. But how could Joy look at him and not know something was wrong?

From what Larry had said, she wasn't herself. She was probably so absorbed in whatever was bothering her that she hadn't noticed Larry was suffering, too. Mitch could think of two things that might be bothering her. Either she was afraid Larry would find out about the affair. Or she was afraid of what the police would uncover in their investigation.

As for Larry, he'd convinced himself that Joy's involvement in the affair had not been voluntary. Almost. There was still a part of him that feared what she'd say if he asked her about Thornton. Mitch suspected that was the real reason he'd said nothing. He wondered what would be worse than hearing from your wife's own lips that she'd fallen in love with another man.

The answer was immediately forthcoming.

"If Joy—" Larry said, "if she's done something...it's not her fault. He drove her to it."

No wonder Larry hadn't been sleeping or bothering to shave. He was fully occupied with the desperate fear that his wife had murdered Graham Thornton.

"It had to be what they call extenuating circumstances, Chief," Larry said, still trying to convince Mitch—and himself. "Have you talked to her?"

"Briefly. She claims she doesn't know anything about the murder."

His worried expression didn't ease. "Do we need to get a lawyer?"

"No, not yet."

"Can I go now?"

Mitch nodded and watched Larry Yeaky place some coins on the table and leave the café with slumped shoulders. Dicey materialized from the kitchen, came to the booth, and pocketed the coins. "You two looked like you were having a mightly serious conversation."

Nosiness was second nature to the waitresses who worked at the Three Squares. A new bit of gossip made their day, gave them something to pass along to their customers besides what was on the menu.

"That so, Dicey?" Through the front window of the café, Mitch watched a dark-green BMW drive up and park. He made a move to leave but sank back down when he saw who got out of the BMW. "Dicey, I think I'll have that cup of coffee after all."

She left, clearly disappointed at not having gotten an inkling of what Mitch and Larry Yeaky had talked about. Cara Thornton came into the café and looked around. Mitch caught her eye and waved. "Join me?"

Cara hesitated a moment, then shrugged off her coat, hung it on the rack, and came to the booth. "Is this how you earn your pay, Chief Bushyhead?"

"You'd be surprised what I learn here."

Cara's smile seemed forced. Dicey brought Mitch's coffee, looking Cara over curiously. She didn't seem to know who Cara was. As Mitch would have guessed,

Cara didn't make a habit of frequenting the Three Squares, or probably any other eating establishment in Buckskin.

"What can I get you, miss?" Dicey asked.

Cara looked up at the waitress. "Decaffeinated coffee—if it's not instant. Or is that too much to ask for?"

"We brew all our coffee, miss," Dicey said a bit snappily as she left.

"I hate this town."

"You're not planning to be around here long, are you?"

"You can bet on that."

"Leaving the country?"

"You can bet on that, too." This was said with great ferocity. Somebody was putting stumbling blocks in Cara's way. Maybe her mother hadn't crumbled so easily after all. "Even if I have to go alone."

"I thought your fiancé was going with you."

Her eyes flashed blue fire. "All of a sudden, Michael's Mister Serious. Says he can't do anything until he's finished med school *and* his residency. It might not look good on his record. All this time, he's let me think he'd go, but now that Mother's agreed, it's another story. He never intended to go, the creep. He never thought I'd get the money."

Mitch wondered if the fiancé had ever actually said he'd go, or if Cara was so used to getting her way, she'd never imagined any other outcome. "Have you thought about waiting and using the money for a honeymoon?"

"Wait six years? No way. I'm getting out of here, with or without Michael." She was distracted for a moment by the waitress setting her coffee in front of her. Then she said, "Maybe I can still talk him into going."

Poor Michael, Mitch thought. But he wasn't really interested in the fiancé. "I was out at the lodge yesterday. Magda's working with your mother now."

"Mother told me all about it. She's always liked Magda. Don't ask me why."

"What did Magda ever do to you?"

"Nothing, really. I've just never liked her attitude. When she and Graham were first married, she was going to be the big peacemaker, force me and Graham to like each other. She ingratiated herself with Mother and Daddy, but it didn't work with me. She was always inviting me to dinner. When I told her to get off my back, she had the nerve to call me a spoiled brat. I guess she found out what Graham was really like, though. I almost felt sorry for her a few times."

Mitch thought of the bruises Larry Yeaky had seen on his wife's arms. "I've heard your brother could get physical."

Cara looked at him sharply. "He didn't do it with me. He never dared."

He was a thoroughly detestable man, Magda had said. When Mitch had asked how her husband had reacted when she confronted him about other women, she hesitated. *It was—unpleasant*. But there had been rage deep in her eyes.

"He beat Magda?"

"I never saw him do it, and you can bet Graham would hit her where her clothes would cover the evidence."

"But you still think she was battered."

"It was something I wondered about. Once, when I went by their house, she was wearing a halter. There was an old, yellow bruise in the middle of her back. That's a weird place to bruise yourself. I asked her how she did it. She gave me a strange look and walked away.''

Maybe Duck was right, Mitch reflected. Maybe Magda was the perp. On the other hand, he only had Cara's word that Graham hadn't raised his fist to her. If she'd made him angry enough, maybe by threatening to testify that he was a wife beater to help Magda in the divorce case... Mitch could envision Cara doing that, to force her brother to give her money from her trust fund.

He wanted to talk to Magda Thornton again. ''I'd better get on back to the station, Cara. I'll get your coffee.'' He dropped a dollar bill and two quarters on the table.

''Thanks.''

She seemed deep in thought as he left. No doubt working on another tack to take with the fiancé.

TWENTY

EMILY BUTTONED HER COAT up to her chin. Underneath, she was wearing both of the shirts she'd brought with her. Unable to pull on one pair of jeans over the other, she'd rolled the extra pair and stuffed them into one of the deep side pockets of her coat, her dirty underwear in the other.

It was after five and getting dark. Kevin and Temple still hadn't come to rescue her. She'd waited this long, hoping the strong wind that had come up after noon would die. It hadn't, but she simply could not stay in the lake house another night. She would have to borrow a telephone and call Temple. If she couldn't reach either Temple or Kevin, she'd have to walk.

She looked around the living room to make sure she'd left it as she'd found it. She'd already stored the quilt and the electric heater in the closet, and everything else looked okay.

In the kitchen, she pulled a trash bag from the box she'd noticed earlier. She dropped in the remainder of the bread, bologna, and cheese she'd purchased at the convenience store before leaving town. She looked at the two remaining cans of soup for a moment, wondering if she could leave them. The Robertses had left several cans of food in the cabinet but no soup. She'd better get rid of them, too. She stuffed the soup cans into the trash bag.

She put on her earmuffs and gloves and went out the back door to leave the bag in the trash can for pickup.

She checked to make sure the house key was in her pocket, then locked the door behind her.

When she stepped off the sheltered deck, the wind caught the trash bag and almost wrenched it from her hands. She grabbed it and, turning her back to the wind, shuffled sideways to the trash can. It sat in a wired enclosure anchored by thick posts at the four corners; otherwise the can would have been whipped away long ago. Emily wrestled open the hinged lid, shoved the bag inside, and pushed the lid down until she heard it snap.

She had to walk, facing the wind, to the house next door. It was dark enough to have a lamp on, but she didn't see any lights. She'd knock on the door just to be sure no one was home before she tried another house. The house was several hundred yards from the Robertses' place, but all the other houses were even farther away than this one.

Stuffing her gloved hands into her pockets, she leaned into the wind and headed for the back entrance because it was the closest. The wind numbed her face before she reached the driveway. A night-light shone over the double garage, and she peered in through a glass pane. No cars. Her heart sank, and she hesitated in front of the garage for a moment. There could still be someone inside, she told herself, and made for the back porch.

For a full minute she stood on the porch, sheltered from the wind by a wing on the north side of the house. She knocked several times, but she heard nothing from inside. Still reluctant to leave the comparative comfort of the porch, she opened the storm screen and tried the door, knowing that she wouldn't be brave enough to go in, even if she found it unsecured. But it was locked.

Well. Back into the wind. She had started down the porch steps when the headlights of a car threw light down the driveway from the side street. Thank goodness. The neighbor was coming home.

Emily waited until the car turned into the garage and someone came out and walked toward the back entrance. Emily moved farther down the steps into the edge of the circle of light from the lamp over the garage. "Hello."

The neighbor hesitated, sizing her up, then walked toward her, head bent against the wind. "May I help you?"

"I was wondering if I could use your phone."

The neighbor stepped past her to unlock the door. "I don't believe I know you. Do you live around here?"

"Oh, no—my name's Emily." She didn't want to give her last name unless she had to. The neighbor might connect it with her father and phone him to ask why his daughter was wandering around, alone, this far from town.

The door opened. "Come on in, Emily."

They entered a large kitchen—dark wood cabinets, gleaming appliances with smoked glass doors, foot-square, blue ceramic tiles on the floor. A square, butcher-block table stood in the center of the U formed by the cabinets, copper pots hanging from a rack over it. Everything looked very expensive. Not surprisingly. All the year-round homes in Lakeview were large and probably cost a small fortune. Emily was impressed.

The neighbor, coatless now, was running water into a teakettle. "Sit down. I'll make hot tea. You look frozen."

The feeling was coming back into Emily's face, and it stung. "I don't want to be any bother. Really, I just need to use your phone."

"Where do you live?"

Emily knew she couldn't get away with saying she was from the neighborhood. The neighbor had already said Emily wasn't familiar. "In town." The neighbor was eyeing her suspiciously. "I've been staying next door in the Robertses' house."

"Alone?"

"Uh—well, yes."

"You look too young to live alone."

"Oh, no. I don't live alone. I was doing a favor for the parents of a friend." Emily realized that explained nothing. No wonder the neighbor was suspicious. She shouldn't have said she'd been staying next door, but it was too late now. "Only for a couple of days," she added, "while—" While what? It got worse and worse. "Painting." She stammered. "I've been painting the living room—for some spending money, you know."

Narrowed eyes told her she wasn't a very good liar. Fortunately the kettle whistled then, and those suspicious eyes were averted.

The silence seemed to Emily to shout "Liar!" She searched for something else to talk about—if she changed the subject, perhaps she wouldn't have to say any more about why she'd been next door. "Is Nila Ridge a friend of yours?"

"Why do you ask?" the neighbor said without turning around.

"I saw her come to this house—night before last. I knew who she was because I've seen her with her boys. The older one's a grade behind me in school."

"I see."

"I thought she must be a friend because she stayed so long." Emily realized too late that it sounded as though she'd been spying on the house. "I heard her car leave. This is such a quiet neighborhood, you notice things like that."

"Yes, Nila's a friend of mine," the neighbor replied, turning around now. "Why don't you take your coat off and sit down. I'll cut you a piece of walnut cake to go with the tea."

Emily didn't want to seem ungrateful. And the cake was tempting. She hadn't eaten anything since the cheese-and-bologna sandwich at noon. She would be able to hear Kevin's car if he and Temple arrived while she was in the house. "Well, okay. Thank you."

"Hang your coat in the utility room—right through that door."

The warmth of the kitchen was comforting. It was nice to talk to someone—anyone—after the isolation of the past two days. What difference could five minutes make? Obediently, Emily went into the next room and hung her coat on one of the pegs along one wall. She stuffed her gloves into the pocket with the jeans and hooked her earmuffs over another peg. She straightened her clothes and finger-combed her hair before returning to the kitchen.

Two cups of tea and a thick slab of dark, moist-looking cake were arranged on the small, white wrought iron table in a corner of the kitchen. The neighbor was already sitting in one of the wrought iron chairs, sipping tea.

Emily pulled out the other chair. "This looks wonderful. I didn't realize I was hungry until you mentioned the cake."

"It's my own recipe. I won a competition with it a few years ago."

"What was the prize?"

"A thousand dollars."

Emily cut a bite, eager to taste a cake that was worth a thousand dollars. It was sweet and rich and crunchy with walnuts and raisins. "It's delicious."

"Thank you." The neighbor was smiling but watching Emily carefully at the same time. She wondered if she was suspected of being up to no good. Looking the place over for a future burglary. What did they call it? Casing the joint.

The hot tea was soothing, tasting of exotic herbs and almonds. It seemed to warm Emily all the way down to her toes. She realized she was eating too fast—she was not merely hungry, she was ravenous. Not wanting to appear gluttonous, she slowed down and began to cut dainty pieces and laid her fork down between bites.

A clock chimed in another part of the house. "I really appreciate your kindness," Emily said. "I'll finish this and make my call and get out of your hair."

"Take your time. Would you like another cup of tea?"

"Well—I really don't . . . all right."

The neighbor was already up, coming back to the table with a ceramic teapot. "I'd be glad to drive you to town myself."

"Oh, no. Thank you, but I've been enough of a nuisance already. I'll call my friend." Emily could see no phone in the kitchen. There was probably one in the hall that led from the kitchen deeper into the house. The hall was too dark to tell exactly where or how far it went.

"It's no trouble. I'd planned to go in anyway."

Emily's tongue was beginning to feel funny. Sort of numb. She wondered if she was allergic to one of the herbs in the tea. She felt a little drowsy, too. Probably because this was the first time she'd truly relaxed all day. She blinked hard to rid her eyelids of their sudden desire to droop.

"You don't look at though you've been sleeping very well."

"I haven't. The house was cold, even with a heater. I didn't think it would be."

"But you stuck it out, finished the job. That's admirable."

Job? What...oh, yes. She'd said she was painting the living room. "Thank you." Gee, she was sleepy. "I really need to get to town."

"Of course." The neighbor jumped up and carried the cups and empty dessert plate to the sink. "Wait here while I run upstairs and get something I need to take with me. I'll only be a minute."

A few minutes later, Emily heard the sound of steps on the stairs. It seemed to come from a great distance. Of course, this was a big house. Maybe she ought to try to call Temple before they left. Or Kevin. So they'd know what had become of her if they arrived at the lake house before she got home and had a chance to call from there.

She pushed back her chair and tried to stand, staggered, and caught the tabletop to keep from falling. Her head felt as though it was full of wool. This was more than being sleepy. She must be coming down with something. She heard a telephone ring twice, then stop as it was picked up.

She sank back into her chair. Couldn't call anyone now, anyway. Besides, it seemed too much effort to go in search of the nearest extension. Temple and Kevin would just have to wonder, if they missed one other. Serve them right for making her wait so long.

She'd put her head down on the table, only for a minute.

AFTER LEAVING THE CAFÉ, Mitch started the engine and heater in the patrol car. Hesitating, he left the gear selector in park instead of going to reverse and sat for a few minutes, thinking.

Before talking to Cara in the café, he'd never heard even a hint that Graham Thornton was a wife beater. Everybody said he had a nasty temper. Few people seemed to have liked him. But there were a lot of men who were a pain in the neck; that didn't mean they went home and battered their wives. If it was true, Doc Sullivan might know. But he'd consider it confidential information.

Everyone is a moon, and has a dark side which he never shows to anybody. Twain and Millicent Kirkwood were, no doubt, right about that. Would Magda admit it? He'd given her plenty of opportunity the last time they talked, and she hadn't even suggested such a thing. But there had been that rage in her eyes.

Even if Magda did admit it, would he be any closer to solving the case? She'd kicked Graham out months ago. But did that necessarily mean the battering had stopped? If they'd argued over the divorce settlement, and he'd seen red . . .

Derring would know, too. Mitch sighed. Derring was less likely than Doc Sullivan to tell her anything, except to stuff it. Doc would be more polite, but it would come down to the same thing. And Cara wasn't exactly an unbiased informant. She disliked Magda, had hated Graham. She'd covered herself, said she'd never seen a battering with her own eyes. She'd just tossed out the suggestion. She could even be trying to muddy the waters, if she was implicated in the murder. Hard to tell what was going on in that pretty, conniving head.

What about Joy Yeaky? Her own husband thought she'd killed Graham Thornton. But Joy might have gotten those bruises on her arms in any number of ways. His mind veered suddenly on a new trail. What if there were no bruises? What if Larry was laying the groundwork for a defense if Joy was arrested? Maybe she had even confessed to him. Maybe they were in it together.

A lot of *what if*'s and *maybe*'s. He'd start with Magda. Glancing at his watch, he realized he'd been in the café longer than he'd thought. It was almost six. He'd go back to the station first and see if Duck and Roo had picked up anything helpful out at Lakeview.

TWENTY-ONE

DUCK AND ROO arrived back at the station minutes after Mitch did. Virgil and Mitch were in Mitch's office, where Mitch was filling Virgil in on his conversations with Larry Yeaky and Cara Thornton when the other two officers appeared in the open doorway. Both looked cold and discouraged.

Duck took off his coat and slumped in the nearest chair, rubbing his hands together to warm them. "Nobody out there saw anything," he grumbled. "We've wasted the better part of two days, freezing our asses off."

Roo kept his coat on. His freckled face was mottled from the cold. His nose was red and running. He pulled out a crumpled handkerchief and blew into it. "We never did find anybody at home at about twelve houses. I wrote down the addresses, if you want us to keep checking back, Chief."

"What about Magda Thornton?"

"We saw the lights on in her house as we were leaving Lakeview," Duck said. "She couldn't have been home long because we'd already checked twice this afternoon. We stopped and talked to her. She hadn't seen Nila Ridge in the neighborhood either."

"At least that's what she says," Roo put in.

"You don't believe her?" Mitch asked.

Roo shrugged and began taking off his coat. "She acted pissed."

"She wouldn't invite us into the house," Duck said. "Made us stand on the porch in the wind and yell at her through the storm door."

"She said she'd already talked to you earlier today," Roo said, "and if she'd known anything about Nila Ridge's disappearance, she'd have told you then."

"Then she slammed the door in our faces."

"She's got a For Sale sign in her yard," Roo added.

"She can't afford to keep the house," Mitch said. "I think she'll sell her interest in the lodge, too. She's eager to get away from Buckskin."

"Probably without leaving a forwarding address," Virgil mused. "Duck, I'm beginning to think you've been right all along. She could be our murderer."

"Yeah, but we don't have the evidence to arrest her."

"It's a toss-up between Magda and Joy Yeaky, as far as I'm concerned," Mitch said. "But Magda's tougher. The only way we'll ever make a case against Magda Thornton is to break her, get a confession."

Roo snorted. "Good luck."

Mitch looked at the phone on his desk, then decided against an advance notice of his arrival. He rose and grabbed his coat. "Virgil, you might fill them in on what we've been talking about before they go home. I'll write up the reports tomorrow. I'm going out to Lakeview now to talk to Magda Thornton. Then I'll corner Joy at the lodge. Maybe if we keep up the pressure..." He left the office with his sentence unfinished.

Before Mitch reached the outskirts of the town, Virgil's voice pierced the static on the radio. "BPD One, this is BPD Two. Come in."

Mitch plucked the speaker from its hook. "This is BPD One. Go ahead."

"We have a body east of town. Can you pick me up?"

Mitch stifled his urgency to know more details. There were a few police-band radios in town, and he didn't want some busybody beating them to the body. He checked his rearview mirror, U-turned the patrol car, and sped back to the station via a little-traveled street.

As soon as Mitch pulled up behind the station house, Virgil stepped out and got in. "It's a woman," he said. "You turn north four miles east of town on Highway 10."

That was less than two miles east of the lodge. "Who called it in?"

"Nolan Chase."

"I don't know him."

"He's Burton Chase's oldest son. He'd be about forty. Last I heard he was living in Texas somewhere."

"I didn't think there were any houses out that way."

"He said he's been staying with his dad and working in Muskogee. He didn't mention his wife. Maybe they're divorced."

"Burton Chase lives farther out than that."

"Nolan said he was coon hunting in those woods east of the lodge last night. When he got ready to leave, he couldn't call up one of his dogs. Today, when he got home from work, the dog still hadn't shown up. So he went back to look for him."

"Where did he call from?"

"His dad's. The lodge was closer, but he said he didn't think about that until later. He sort of panicked, I guess."

"Stumbling over a dead body in the woods can do that to you."

"Yeah. Nolan said he'd meet us about a mile down the road, after the turn off the highway."

"Did he recognize the woman?"

"Didn't say, but I doubt it. It was dark and he was using a flashlight. He said she was facedown. He didn't disturb the body."

"Didn't he even check her pulse?"

"All he said was he was sure she was dead."

Shortly after they left the highway, the patrol car's headlights picked up an old GMC pickup parked at the side of the road. Mitch stopped behind it and took his flashlight from the glove compartment. The two men in the pickup got out and stood in the road. They wore fleece-lined denim jackets and stocking caps pulled down over their ears.

"Hello, Mr. Chase," Mitch said, shaking the old man's hard, rough hand.

"Chief. Virgil. This is my boy, Nolan."

The younger man was a head taller than his father, but he had the same hawk nose and prominent chin. "She's in the woods there a ways. I almost didn't see her. Somebody had covered her up with dead leaves, but I smelled her." Nolan Chase paused to swallow hard. "I uncovered her just enough to see that it's a woman."

"Lead the way," Mitch said.

"Why don't you wait in the truck for me, Dad?"

The older man hesitated only a moment before acquiescing with a curt nod of his head. Nolan turned on his flashlight, and Mitch and Virgil followed him into the woods.

"I'm glad he didn't argue," Nolan said when they'd gone a short way. "He's already had two heart attacks. I didn't even want him to come back with me, but he insisted."

"Last I heard, you were living in Texas," Virgil said.

They trudged single file through layers of dead leaves. The knowledge of what waited for them in the dark woods made the sound of their footsteps seem eerie. "I got laid off six months ago. My wife and I are divorced, and my daughter's in college in New Jersey. So I came back to stay with Dad. He's alone and not well, though he's usually too stubborn to admit it." They walked a way in silence. Then Nolan stopped abruptly. "I don't know if I can go any closer without getting sick. That smell."

Mitch could smell the corpse now, too. It was frigid right now, but yesterday the temperature had been high enough for decomposition to set in. Virgil had pulled out his handkerchief and held it over his nose and mouth.

"She's right in front of you, about three hundred yards."

"Wait for us here," Mitch said. He pulled out his own handkerchief, and he and Virgil walked on.

The body was lying half under a massive clump of gnarled vines. Slender calves and ankles and small feet in rubber-soled, lace-up oxfords extended from beneath the vines. A dark coat was twisted around the legs beginning at mid-calf. Leaves were piled to one side of the legs.

Keeping his handkerchief pressed to his nose with one hand, Mitch said, "Help me pull her out." He gripped one foot, Virgil the other, and easily pulled the body clear of the vines.

Straightening, Mitch played the beam of the flashlight over the body. The corpse's dark hair was matted with leaves and dried blood. She had been shot in the back of the head with a small-caliber bullet. A larger caliber would have taken half the head off. Mitch turned the body over and heard Virgil's breath escape with a soft curse.

"Oh, hell . . . I kept hoping . . ."

Neither man was surprised, but Mitch had been hoping, too. Hoping it would be a stranger, somebody passing through, somebody who didn't have two fatherless young boys waiting for her to come home to them.

The coat gapped open in front, exposing the brown uniform worn by the housekeeping employees of Eagle's Nest Lodge. Nila Ridge had gone directly from work Tuesday evening to meet her killer.

TWENTY-TWO

THE CHASES HAD GONE HOME and phoned for an ambulance. The ambulance had come and returned to town with Nila Ridge's body. Since there was no one else at the station, Virgil hitched a ride with the driver after sketching a diagram of the crime scene. It was too dark to explore the scene tonight. Mitch would return early the next day.

He sat alone in his patrol car now on the country road, closed his eyes, and rested his head for a moment on the back of the car seat. Emily would be looking for him to drive up to the Robertses' house any minute. Well, she'd be okay until he got there. He couldn't think about it now.

He contemplated what he had to do; it was the part of his job that he found the most distressing. He had to tell Mrs. Redeagle that her daughter was dead. This was bad enough, but Nila's mother and sons would not even have the small consolation of knowing that she'd died after a long illness, that everything medical science could do for her had been done—or that she'd died accidentally but instantly, with no suffering, no time to know what had befallen her.

She had died violently and probably with full knowledge of her impending death. Nila wouldn't have agreed to meet the killer in the woods. Even though she had misjudged the murderer's reaction to her demand for money in exchange for her silence. Mitch was sure that's what had happened, as sure of it as of any aspect of the case. It was the only way to account for the phone call made in secrecy last Friday night. That phone call had resulted in Nila's murder.

Driven by desperation into probably the first illegal act of her life, frightened and alert for a sign that her scheme wasn't going to work, she would surely have been suspicious if a meeting in a woods was suggested. She would have insisted on meeting in a place that she considered safe, yet where she wouldn't be observed talking to somebody who might later be exposed as a murderer.

Wherever that meeting took place, she'd been brought to the woods later. If she was killed before being dumped there, she at least would have had less time to be aware that she was traveling to her death. If she was killed in the woods, she would have been brought there forcibly, terrified, perhaps pleading for her life. Tomorrow's investigation of the crime scene might reveal whether she'd been killed there or was brought there afterward.

In any case, she'd no doubt had time to know that she'd made a terrible mistake in attempting to blackmail Graham Thornton's killer. Mrs. Redeagle would have to deal with that while making decisions concerning the future of her grandsons.

If Mitch's reasoning was correct, she'd also have to deal with knowing that the body had lain in the woods since sometime Tuesday night. Three days and nights in the dark woods, beneath a thin blanket of leaves. When they had lifted the corpse into a body bag, Mitch had seen the hand that had been pinned beneath her when he rolled her over. The flesh had been torn away. Sometime within the last few hours, a scavenger had discovered the body. The mortician would hide the hand beneath the coffin blanket. Perhaps Mrs. Redeagle would never have to know about the scavenger.

The interior of the patrol car had had time to grow quite cold, but Mitch sat there for another few moments, coat collar pulled up and hands stuffed in his pockets, dreading what he must yet do that night before he could go home.

Faces rose and faded behind his lowered lids: Julian Moncrief's, arrogant; Joy Yeaky's, tearful and frightened; Larry Yeaky's, anguished; Cara Thornton's, petulant and determined; LaDonna Thornton's, stunned and disbelieving; Magda Thornton's aloof and controlled. And one of them was a killer.

Everyone is a moon, and has a dark side which he never shows to anybody. What dark sides were these people hiding? If he knew that, he would probably know who had murdered Graham Thornton and Nila Ridge.

On the face of it, Joy Yeaky now seemed to have had the most to gain by Thornton's death. On the very day he died, Thornton had refused to end their affair, according to Joy. On the same day, Larry Yeaky had heard of the affair from another source. Passion was behind most murders, and the people whose lives were involved with Graham Thornton's had strong feelings about the man. Fear in Joy's case, and in Larry's rage. Neither Cara nor Magda had made any bones about the fact that they hated Thornton. Julian Moncrief had not been a fan of Thornton's either, but killing a man for giving you a bad job reference seemed an extreme reaction for a sane person. The chef was certainly sane. Mitch was inclined to drop Moncrief from his list of suspects.

That left Joy, Larry, Cara, and Magda. Nila had known something about the murder, and she'd used it to try to blackmail one of them. Which one?

The Yeakys seemed unlikely candidates. Larry's van was worth practically nothing. They lived in a rented house. They had the Bronco, but Mitch would bet they'd be paying on it for another two or three years. The only money they had coming in was Joy's paycheck. Would Nila have taken such a risk for the small amount the Yeakeys could scrape together—a few hundred at most? Mitch didn't think so. Cara and Magda were far better prospects for blackmail.

A piece of dead tree limb, flung by a sudden gust of wind, scraped across the patrol car's windshield. The patrol car rocked a little with the strength of it. Mitch opened his eyes, all at once aware that his toes were starting to grow numb from the cold.

Before he went back to town to call on Nila Ridge's mother, he'd do what he'd started out to do when Virgil's radio message had altered his course. He wanted to see Magda Thornton's face when he told her that Nila's body had been found.

SOMEONE WAS GRIPPING Emily's arm, trying to pull her to her feet. She tried to open her eyes, but they were too heavy. She was heavy all over. She felt as though she'd been cast in bronze. And her head was swimming. Oh, she felt so sick.

"Come on. Get on your feet."

The voice was far away. Why couldn't they let her alone? But, no, she was being dragged from her chair. She staggered against something hard—a table?—and pain stabbed her side. Somebody caught her from behind.

Was this what it felt like to be drunk? In her entire life, she couldn't remember ever drinking any alcohol, but there seemed to be a number of things she couldn't remember. Wasn't she supposed to meet Temple and Kevin, or had she dreamed it? Where was she? How had she come to be there?

"Can't walk," Emily mumbled.

"Yes, you can. I'll help you. That's it."

Someone was propelling her forward, forcing her feet to keep pace. "Sleep . . . please."

"Soon."

Emily managed to force her eyes open. There was a hazy impression of kitchen cabinets and a door ajar before the effort of keeping her lids raised was too much.

"Stairs here. Step down."

She stumbled and would have fallen if she hadn't slammed against something hard at waist level. A banister, she thought foggily, when a hand grabbed her hand and placed it on something solid, cold, and down-slanting.

"A few more steps."

"Where . . . going?"

"Where you can rest. Don't worry. Everything will be all right."

Rest. That's what she wanted.

"Here we are."

Hands pressed down on her shoulders, but something caught her fall. A bed. Then she was lying down. Somebody was covering her. Sighing, she snuggled down beneath the covers. Mmmm—she was so sleepy.

In her last moment of consciousness—or in a dream—she heard, far away, the sound of a key turning in a lock. Then she knew nothing.

TWENTY-THREE

MITCH DROVE another quarter mile slowly down the graveled road, searching for he knew not what in the beam of the headlights—something, anything, that might give him a clue to the murderer. There were no clearly visible footprints or tire tracks, but the road had a rock bed covered by a thin scattering of gravel. Car tires probably wouldn't leave much of an impression, footsteps none at all. He'd check again tomorrow. Maybe something would show up by daylight.

Sighing, he swung as far to the right as the trees allowed and made a tight U-turn. As the patrol car's headlights swept the trees on the opposite side of the road, Mitch saw the flash of light reflected on metal. He stopped and got out, leaving the headlights on.

Flashlight in hand, he entered the woods. A car was hidden in the trees less than a hundred yards from the road. He played the beam over the license plate. Nila Ridge's tag number.

He switched the flashlight to his left hand and, pulling his gun from its holster, he circled around to the driver's side of the car. It appeared to be empty. His flashlight beam illuminated the front and back seats. Nobody. Nothing. The driver's door was unlocked. He opened it and checked the glove compartment and the floor in front and back. The glove compartment contained a folded map of Oklahoma and a maintenance manual, while the floor gave up nothing but a few gum wrappers.

Mitch holstered his gun, closed the car door, and leaned forward against the hood for an instant. In her own car, Nila had driven, or been driven, to her death. Who had sat beside her? Who had marched Nila into the woods on the other side of the road, killed her, covered her hurriedly with leaves, and left the scene on foot?

Mitch retraced his steps to the patrol car. All at once beset by a sense of urgency, he drove as fast as he dared to the highway and turned back toward the lodge and Lakeview.

Soft light shone through the gauzy white draperies covering Magda Thornton's front windows. Mitch punched the doorbell and heard chimes echoing inside the house. Quick footsteps were muffled by carpeting. The door opened.

"Good evening."

"Well." She stood in the doorway in white wool slacks and sweater, framed attractively by the light behind her, and stared at him. "It's our dedicated police chief. Isn't it a bit late to be disturbing law-abiding citizens?"

"Would you mind inviting me in?"

"Yes, if you want the truth. But I suppose I must cooperate or be accused, again, of covering up my involvement in my husband's murder. For the record, I'm quite aware that I'm not required to permit an invasion of my privacy simply because I find you on my doorstep." She turned and, leaving the door open, walked away, leaving Mitch to open the screen door and follow her.

He saw her disappear into the living room as he closed the heavy inner door. A single table lamp provided the only light in the room. She was standing in front of the stone fireplace, her sweater and slacks blending into the white stone facade so that it was difficult to tell where one ended and the other began. But her red hair, hanging in loose, layered waves to her shoulders, stood out in stark contrast like glistening copper. She didn't offer him a chair. She folded her arms in front of her and waited for him to speak.

"How are things at the lodge?"

"Could we skip the social chitchat? I've had a long, frustrating day. I hate the damn lodge, not a criminal offense, as far as I'm aware."

She seemed calm, but her eyes glittered with suppressed anger. "Do you remember where you were Tuesday evening?" Mitch asked delicately.

"Oh, good Lord. I'm not senile. I was right here. Where else would I be?"

"When did you arrive home?"

"Six o'clock, give or take a few minutes. I've been over all of this with your officers. The whole Buckskin police force seems to have descended on our quiet neighborhood. Frankly, we're all pretty sick of uniformed men traipsing across our yards."

"I would appreciate it if you would go over it one more time."

She tossed back her hair, taking all ten red-tipped fingers through it, a muscle in her tight angry jaw working. "Officer Duckworth can't read his notes?"

"Please."

A heavy sigh. "Very well, Chief. I worked at the lodge until a quarter of six. I drove home, ate a light supper—" A scornful curl of red lips. "Do you want the menu?"

"That's not necessary."

"Glory be. Where was I? Oh, yes. I ran a hot tub and soaked for twenty or thirty minutes. Then I went to bed with a novel that came from my book club in Tuesday's mail. A mystery featuring a bumbling detective. Would you like to see it?"

"No. Did you see anyone that evening, talk to anyone on the telephone?"

"No and no."

"You didn't notice anyone in the neighborhood, behaving in an uncharacteristic way—or someone who doesn't live here?"

"I didn't notice anyone period. Let me spell it out for you. The only time I saw Nila Ridge on Tuesday was in the early afternoon when she was cleaning the offices. I don't know the woman. I've never spoken more than five words to her. I have no knowledge of her private life, nor do I have the slighest interest in acquiring any. I do not know or care why she's gone missing or where she might be."

"Nila is no longer missing."

"Oh? Then why are you here, badgering me about Tuesday evening?"

"About an hour ago, a coon hunter, searching for a lost hound, found Nila's body in the woods east of the lodge. Somebody had done a piss-poor job of burying her." With a sudden burst of frustrated anger, he added viciously, "The back of her head is a bloody mess and a scavenger had been feasting on her left hand."

"Dear God!" She gasped at him, the scorn in her eyes fading into shock, or a good imitation thereof. "What on earth has this to do with me?"

"I am investigating a double murder. Everyone connected to either of the victims will be questioned."

"You think this Indian woman's death—"

"Murder," Mitch corrected quietly.

"Yes, murder. You think it's connected to Graham's."

"That's a logical supposition, don't you agree?"

"No." She moved to one of the mauve armchairs flanking the fireplace and sat down. "She was hardly Graham's type, if that's what you're insinuating."

"She was his employee. She worked at the lodge five days a week. She saw what went on there."

She looked up at him curiously. "But he'd fired her. She might have, understandably, wanted to kill him. Maybe she did, for all I know. But then, who..."

"Who killed her? Yes, that is the question, isn't it? I think it was the same person who killed your husband."

She stared at him, and for the first time he saw fear in her brown eyes. "You think *I* did it?"

"I don't know. But it was someone who was familiar with the layout of the lodge, someone who thought they could get in and out of your husband's suite without being seen. Unfortunately, Nila saw or heard something. She called the killer last Friday night and asked for money in exchange for keeping silent. I guess it took her a week to work up the nerve. A meeting was set up for Tuesday evening."

"And she was...killed." Her glance flitted fearfully around the room as though she feared the elegant setting might dissolve, and her along with it, at any moment. "You said her head...how...?"

"A gunshot. I'll know more of the details in a day or two. Do you have access to a gun, Mrs. Thornton?"

"I've never touched a gun in my life!"

Which doesn't exactly answer my question, Mitch thought. "Never even wanted to?" he asked.

She shook her head.

"Not even when your husband beat you?"

He could see something crumbling behind her eyes. She seemed to wilt into the chair, the erect shoulders slumping, the proud head falling back against the chair for support. Even then, her distress did not erase her cool beauty. Suddenly the brown eyes glittered with unshed tears. She gazed at him and asked, "How did you find out about that?"

Mitch said nothing.

"Cara. It was Cara, wasn't it?"

Mitch still said nothing. He could see her agitation building, and he waited for it to force the truth from her mouth.

"She had no right to talk to anyone about that."

Mitch watched her closely, not moving so much as a finger.

"I didn't know him—before we were married. Not really. I didn't know he'd grown up with it, for as far back as he could remember. They kept it hidden, all of them, the little family secret that no one ever talked about." She stopped suddenly, her lips pressed tightly together, as if to hold back something. She took a deep breath and brushed the back of her hand across her eyes. "I suppose he just accepted it. That's what men did to their wives when they got out of line."

"Are you saying that Graham's father—?"

Magda's eyes flashed up at him. "Oscar beat La-Donna at least from the time Graham was four years old—that's his earliest memory of hearing them. It probably went on before that. Maybe it started soon after the wedding. I don't know. But it went on until Oscar died."

"Graham told you this?"

"Oh, yes. The first time he hit me—afterward, I mean. He was very contrite. Begged me to forgive him. Promised it wouldn't happen again. I didn't know then that batterers are always sorry afterward. They all promise it won't happen again. After the fourth time, I realized Graham's promises weren't worth the air it took to utter them." She sucked in a quiet, desperate breath.

She seemed to relive the pain of her marriage for a moment. "As I said, after the first time, he tried to justify his actions by telling me about his father. I was in shock. I still couldn't believe what had happened, and I guess that's why I thought it was some kind of aberration, something that could never happen again. Graham said he didn't want to be like Oscar. He said he'd seen his mother's face bruised, her eyes blackened, too many times to count. He'd seen her in such pain she couldn't get out of bed. There had been numerous broken bones, all of which were explained to the doctor who set them as 'accidents.' I think Graham actually hated LaDonna for suffering through it all those years. He hated his father, too. But it changed nothing."

"There's something I don't understand, if what you say is true. Cara idolizes her father. How could she if she'd grown up in a home such as you describe?"

She shook her head wearily. "I don't pretend to understand Cara. I do know that Oscar adored her. Graham said that after Cara got old enough to understand what was going on between her parents, the beatings stopped for a while. Later, Oscar always managed to control his anger until Cara wasn't around. All very calculated. That makes it worse, somehow."

"Cara never actually saw your husband hit you?"

"No... nor her father hit her mother."

"Yet she must have suspected what was happening. Graham told you that LaDonna was sometimes bruised and broken, hurting enough to stay in bed. How could Cara not have known what was going on between her parents?"

"I don't know. Maybe she couldn't admit it to herself."

To keep her father on his pedestal, Mitch thought. Perhaps Magda was right.

"From my own experience, I know that denial is a big part of those sick... sick relationships. Everybody's telling himself it didn't happen or it couldn't be as bad as it seemed at the time."

"You didn't report any of these beatings?"

"To the police?" She hugged herself as though a chill had invaded the room. "No. I never told anyone. I felt so—so humiliated. Lacking in some way. You tell yourself there must be something wrong with you, that you're doing something to bring on the beatings. On the other hand, you know there's something wrong with you for letting it continue. Either way, it's your fault. I don't expect you to understand."

Mitch had seen a lot of things in people and their relationships that he didn't understand. How animals like the Thornton men lived with themselves was one of them. Those dark sides again. "Refresh my memory. When did you separate from your husband?"

"Six—no, seven months ago."

"After you left him, did he ever beat you again?"

Her body grew tense. "He wanted to several times, but I swore I'd call the police if he laid a finger on me. I doubt that I would have, but he believed me."

Did he really? Mitch wondered. Or was she too
ashamed to admit that the battering continued? Too
ashamed, or smart enough to realize that a beating
close to the time of Graham Thornton's murder gave
her an obvious motive. She left him to get away from
the battering. But if it hadn't stopped, even then, how
was a desperate woman, who couldn't bring herself to
seek police protection, to put an end to it?

"He was stalling the divorce," she mused, more to
herself than to Mitch. "He didn't want to give me a
penny." She made a small noise, half sob, half sigh. "I
would have held out as long as necessary, because I
knew he'd never let it go to court where I could testify
about the beatings. But he almost managed to leave me
penniless anyway, didn't he? He might as well have
thrown his money away on the tables in Vegas."

Mitch had three thousand dollars in a money market account, and it was a good month when he could
save a hundred from his salary. He couldn't work up
much sympathy for somebody who had seventy-five
thousand in liquid assets and half interest in Eagle's
Nest Lodge.

"Is there anything else you'd like to tell me before I
leave?" Mitch asked.

She stared at him for an instant. "Graham deserved
to die," she said.

TWENTY-FOUR

GRAHAM DESERVED TO DIE. As Mitch returned to the patrol car, Magda Thornton's statement echoed in his mind. Privately, he might agree with her. Professionally, he was obligated to bring Thornton's killer to trial.

He remembered the bruises Larry Yeaky had seen on his wife's arms. Had there been other hidden bruises on Joy Yeaky's body? Would a man who beat his wife balk at beating other women? Not if he believed he could get away with it, Mitch thought.

Was fragile, pretty Joy Yeaky the murderer? He didn't want it to be Joy. Or Larry. After that scene in Magda Thornton's living room just now, he wasn't fond of the idea of pinning it on her, either. Yet he was getting a strong feeling that he was going to have to arrest one of them. Sometimes a cop's job was worse than torture.

Which reminded him of Nila Ridge's mother and the meeting that couldn't be put off much longer. Since he was this close to the lodge, he decided he'd take a few minutes to question Joy again before calling on Mrs. Redeagle. Then he'd pick up Emily.

He drove back toward the stone-pillared entrance to Lakeview. From there a blacktopped road would take him, by the back way, to the lodge. He drove along the quiet, winding street, sunk in unhappy thoughts. He noticed no other cars on Lakeview's residential streets until headlights reflected in his rearview mirror. The car behind him came up very fast until it was riding his bumper. Deliberately, Mitch slowed down. He hated tailgaters.

The other driver hit his horn. "Back off, pal," Mitch muttered. He didn't want to take the time to pull the other car over, but if the guy insisted . . .

The horn blasted again—and again. "Okay, hotshot," Mitch said, "you asked for it." He turned on his dome light and screeched to a stop. The other car braked abruptly behind him.

Mitch grabbed his ticket pad and climbed out of the patrol car. The driver of the other car was already out, along with a passenger. They ran toward him.

"Chief Bushyhead!" A girl's voice, high and shrill. "Thank goodness, it's you!" It was Temple Roberts. Kevin Hartsbarger was with her. Mitch saw now that the other car was Kevin's Ford.

They stopped in front of Mitch. Now that he could see their faces clearly in the illumination from a streetlight, he realized that something was wrong. Kevin looked frightened and Temple had obviously been crying. He closed his ticket pad. Why wasn't Emily with them? Had she gone back home today? "What's going on?"

"We can't find Emily," Temple blurted.

Mitch's heart jerked. "What do you mean, you can't find her? She's been staying with you, Temple."

"She—" Temple's voice broke. "She was at the lake house. She—oh, I'm sorry I lied to you when you phoned. I'm so worried. It's my fault. . . ."

Mitch gripped the girl's shoulder. "Calm down, Temple. Now. Start at the beginning. Has your family been staying at the lake house?"

"Mr. and Mrs. Roberts don't know anything about it," Kevin said grimly.

Temple hung her head. "They're going to kill me when they find out."

They weren't making any sense. "Temple," Mitch asked, "are you saying that Emily has been staying at the lake house alone?"

She choked back tears. "Yes—just Emily."

"Without your parents' knowledge? I don't believe this."

Temple couldn't reply for crying.

"She gave Emily the key," Kevin said. "Stop bawling, Temple, and tell him."

Temple pulled a wad of tissue from her coat pocket and blew her nose. "She—she said she wanted to be alone—to think—you know? She made me promise I wouldn't tell."

Mitch forced back his rising alarm. "When did she come out here?"

"Tuesday after school," Kevin said.

"She was never at your house at all! Temple, do you know there's a killer loose around here somewhere?" Mitch whirled on Kevin. "And why the hell didn't *you* tell me?"

"He didn't know," Temple wailed. "he's been out of town. Nobody knew but me. Not until an hour ago when I asked Kevin to bring me out here. We were supposed to take Emily back to town. I told her I'd be here earlier, but my mother made me go to Tahlequah with her this morning, and it was after four before I could get her to start back."

Kevin raked a hand through his blond hair. "I knew she was depressed, but I didn't think she'd do something this stupid. Maybe I wasn't very sympathetic."

Damn kids, Mitch thought furiously. "How did she get out here in the first place?"

"I guess she walked," Temple said in a small voice. "She said she would if she had to."

"Maybe she walked back then," Mitch said.

"We didn't see anyone walking near the highway when we drove here," Temple said. "Chief Bushyhead, do you think she could have hitched a ride with someone?"

That was probably what had happened, Mitch told himself, but there was a hard kink of fear in his chest. "I'll find out." He got in the patrol car and radioed Virgil at the station. "Call my house and the Jared Roberts residence," Mitch said. "See if Emily is at either of those places, and get back to me."

Mitch drummed the steering wheel impatiently, glowering at Kevin and Temple, who stood, silent and subdued. They looked very young. "You kids might as well get in the backseat out of the cold," Mitch growled.

Moments later, the radio crackled and Virgil said, "This is BPD Two calling BPD One. Come in."

"BPD One here," Mitch said. "What'd you find out?"

"Nobody answered at your number, and she's not at the Robertses'. They think she's with their daughter. Mrs. Roberts said Kevin Hartsbarger came by about forty-five minutes ago. They assumed Emily was with him. According to the daughter, the three of them were going for a drive."

Mitch threw Temple a glance over his shoulder. "Terrific. Keep trying my number. Call me back if you get an answer." Mitch hung the microphone on its hook. "Where's the lake house again, Temple?"

"On Timberlane, the next street east. Oh, my parents are going to be furious."

"Quit feeling sorry for yourself," Kevin muttered. "Where the hell is Emily?"

We'll find her, Mitch told himself. She'll probably be at home when Virgil tries again. She wouldn't really run away—leave town without telling anyone. Where would she go? What would happen to her? She wouldn't accept a ride with a stranger, would she? God, he had to stop thinking about it.

He turned at the end of the block and headed down Timberlane in the opposite direction. The Robertses' lake house was dark. Mitch wheeled into the drive and braked sharply. "Do you have a key, Temple?"

"Emily has it," Temple said in a muffled voice. "The only other one is on my father's key ring."

"We got in through a back window before," Kevin said. "I had to slit the screen. I can go in that way again and open the front door from inside."

Mitch was staring at the dark house, and the knot in his chest was expanding like a fast-growing malignancy. *Undifferentiated*. They had said the cancer in Ellen's body was undifferentiated—meaning it had spread so quickly that they couldn't pinpoint the original site. In a disconnected flash, he saw Nila Ridge's mutilated body. In his seventeen years as a law officer, he could not remember ever feeling so close to losing his grip. His professionalism had deserted him.

"Do it," he said.

Kevin scrambled out of the car and ran to the back of the house.

"We'll find her, won't we?" Temple murmured from the backseat. Mitch opened the glove compartment and grabbed his flashlight. He got out of the car without offering any assurances. Whimpering, Temple followed.

Moments later, a light went on inside the house and Kevin opened the front door. "She's still not here."

Mitch pushed past the boy and strode quickly through the house, throwing open closets and cabinets. Subdued, Kevin and Temple watched him wordlessly.

When Mitch opened the hall linen closet, Temple ventured, "She must have used those blankets." The blankets were folded and stacked on the floor behind a small electric heater. "Mother always keeps them on the top shelf."

Mitch asked sharply, "Are you sure they were on the shelf?"

"Yes. It means Emily was here. She can't have been gone very long."

"She used that heater," Kevin said. "Come on. I'll show you."

Kevin picked up the heater and carried it to the living room. "See." He pointed at two indentations, about an inch wide and five or six inches long, in the carpet in front of the sofa. He set the heater on the spot. The two legs of the metal stand that held the heater off the floor fitted the impressions perfectly. Evidently Emily had slept on the couch.

She had been here long enough to eat a few meals then. Mitch went into the kitchen. The refrigerator was empty, unplugged. He looked in the cabinet beneath the sink. The plastic trash basket was empty. "Do you have trash cans outside?" he asked Emily.

"In back."

"Come on." They went out through a small utility area behind the kitchen and across a cedar deck. Mitch swung the flashlight beam over the deck and the sloping yard between the deck and the trash cans at the back of the lot. Nothing. Not even a scrap of paper. But there had been a strong north wind earlier; it had eased off a little since, but cold gusts continued to rise and fall around them.

One of the trash cans contained a plastic trash bag. Mitch handed the flashlight to Kevin and, bending, pulled out the bag. Inside were a third of a loaf of bread in a brown-and-yellow store wrapper, an empty chocolate-chip-cookie sack, a box that had held powdered sugar-coated doughnuts, two pieces of bologna, and two unopened cans of chicken-noodle soup. At the bottom of the bag was a wadded brown-paper grocery sack with a cash-register receipt inside. The receipt had Speedy Shop, the name of a convenience store in Buckskin, printed on it, along with a date, 12-19.

"Hey, Chief," Kevin said, "what's this?" He had diverted and lowered the flashlight beam. It shone on a white scrap of cloth snagged in the trash cans' wire enclosure on the north side.

Mitch stuffed the trash bag back into the can and pulled a pair of girls' panties from the wire. They were nylon, bikini style.

"They're Emily's," Temple gasped. "How did they get there?"

A chill that had nothing to do with the weather ran up Mitch's neck. Had Emily been abducted, raped? Please, let her be okay. He felt something at the back of his throat, and he couldn't stop shaking. *Where was she?*

"She might have dropped them when she put out the trash. Did she bring an overnight bag with her?"

"I don't think so," Temple said.

"Maybe she had them in her coat pocket," Kevin said.

Mitch's mind snatched at the suggestion like a drowning man grips a floating log. Let that be what happened, only that.

Mitch grabbed the flashlight from the boy's hand and played the beam over the ground north of the wire enclosure. "If she dropped them on this side of the trash cans, they would have blown against the wire." he walked over the yard north of the trash cans but found nothing else of Emily's. Then the three circled the house, searching the yard in the path of Mitch's flashlight, but they found no other evidence of Emily's presence at the lake house.

They returned to the patrol car, and Mitch radioed the station again. Virgil reported that Mitch's phone still wasn't being answered.

Mitch cursed under his breath and got out of the car again, reluctant to leave the place where Emily had been staying until very recently. He walked down the driveway a few paces, staring into the night.

North of the Roberts place, perhaps five hundred yards, the outline of a much larger house could be seen. There were yard lamps in front and over the garage in back. A string of low-wattage patio lights illuminated the foundation shrubbery. Lights were turned on inside the house, too. Emily would have been able to see this house from the north windows of the Roberts house.

Mitch turned back toward the car. Kevin and Temple were standing beside it, watching him intently, as though expecting him to conjure up Emily from the night. He'd been in that house. He hadn't recognized it immediately because he'd never seen it from this angle before.

"Isn't that LaDonna Thornton's house?"

"Yes," Temple said. "Do you think...oh, maybe she saw Emily!"

"Maybe," Mitch murmured, knowing that it was a long shot. Emily would have taken care not to be seen. "Let's go ask."

As they walked toward the house, a car turned in and followed the driveway to the garage in back. Mitch recognized it as the car Cara Thornton had been driving when he saw her at the Three Squares Cafe that afternoon.

Something fell into place in Mitch's mind. Cara! he thought savagely.

LaDonna Thornton spent long hours at the lodge, leaving Cara in the house alone. It was Cara whom Nila had phoned Friday night. Cara had known her mother would be working late Tuesday night and had arranged a meeting with Nila at her mother's house. Mitch had a horrible premonition. What if Emily had seen Nila and Cara leaving in Nila's car? And what if Cara had discovered that Emily was staying in the Roberts house?

He halted abruptly. "You two wait for me in the car."

"But—" Temple began.

"Do as I say," Mitch ordered harshly. "I don't have time to explain." He hurried toward the Thornton's garage to intercept Cara before she went inside.

He stepped around the corner of the house as she reached the back door. "Cara."

She jumped and dropped her keys. "Good God, you almost scared me into a heart attack! Chief Bushyhead? Why are you lurking out there in the dark?"

"I want to talk to you."

As she bent to pick up her keys, Mitch climbed the back porch steps. His chest was so tight it was an effort to breathe. He wanted to grab her and shake the truth out of her. Get a grip of it, Bushyhead, he told himself. "Where's my daughter?"

"Your daughter!" She looked at him as though he'd lost his mind, and for the first time he sensed something in her—unhappiness? Fear? "What are you talking about? I didn't even know you *had* a daughter." She lifted a key to the lock but couldn't immediately make it fit. She cursed between her teeth, and Mitch grabbed her keys from her hand.

"What do you think you're—"

"I said I want to talk to you." He felt the bolt slide back and opened the door.

"Look, Chief, I don't feel like talking to you right now. I had a terrible row with Michael today and—"

For an instant, Mitch hesitated at the door.

Inside, he told himself. You have to go inside.

What would he find? *Emily, where are you?*

He stopped inside, leaving Cara to follow. In the kitchen, he tossed the keys on the nearest cabinet, wanting to hurl them through a window instead. But he would find out what she knew about Emily faster if he kept his head. In the end, if she refused to talk, he'd tear the place apart.

Cara stormed into the kitchen, grabbed the keys, and stuffed them into her purse. "What is this, the gestapo? You have no right to force your way in here."

Mitch's grip was slipping. "Shut up. My daughter is missing, and I'm in no mood to put up with your crap." Straight ahead, he told himself. Ask her the questions, and don't let your mind stray off track. If he let his thoughts rush ahead, he could only think the worst.

She brushed past him and stalked down a hall. Mitch followed. They entered the large room where he and Doc Sullivan had told LaDonna Thornton that her son was dead. "Mother?" Cara called. There was no answer. She set her purse on a chair and took off her coat. Her face was tight, her blue eyes blazing. "She must be in her room. If she's resting, I don't want to disturb her. We'll go to the study."

The room was walled with books and oak library paneling. A massive walnut desk sat on a muted red-and-blue Oriental rug in the center of the room, facing the door. A brass desk lamp was turned on. Cara switched on the overhead light as well. She didn't close the door. Mitch wondered if she thought she could run for it if she couldn't stonewall him. He unzipped his jacket and stayed where he was, between her and the door.

She walked around the desk and gripped the back of the leather chair. Behind her, wind sighed at the dark window. "I don't know anything about your daughter," she said wearily.

"She's been staying next door in the Roberts house since Tuesday evening. She was probably there until sometime this afternoon."

"I haven't seen anybody around that house. The Robertses only use it during the summer."

"You must have seen a light at night."

"No, I didn't." Her eyes hardened. "I'll bet you're too strict with her. She's run away, hasn't she?"

Mitch held himself together with difficulty. "Here's the way it came down," he said, and there was a crack in his voice. "You and your brother had it out over your trust fund, and he hit you. The same way he dealt with his wife and the woman he was having an affair with."

"That's—"

He overrode her denial, his words like sharp-edged knives. "It must have been the first time anybody ever hit you in your life, but you couldn't give as good as you got. So you decided to kill him. You lived with a diabetic most of your life. You know all about the disease, its treatment, and what can go wrong." She was staring at him now, still and wary and starting to be afraid. "That Monday, you left this house during the snowstorm, went into his suite at the lodge, removed most of the NPH from the bottle Graham was using, and replaced it with enough regular insulin to thrown him into insulin shock. You figured he wouldn't be going out because of the storm, he'd stay in the suite, take his evening insulin injection, go to sleep, and never wake up. The perfect crime—and it almost worked. You came back here and got ready to spend the evening with your fiancé as though nothing unusual had happened. Maybe I don't have all the details down yet, but that's the bare outline.''

She laughed nervously. ''You've flipped out.''

''No, you have, if you think I can't dig up the evidence to convict you.'' He gripped the zippered edges of his jacket until the steel teeth bit into his palms. ''Now, what the hell have you done with my daughter?''

Fear shoved out the anger in her wide eyes. ''Listen to me, you stupid cop. Number one, if Graham had laid a hand on me, I might have killed him. But he didn't. Number two, I've already told you I didn't leave the house at all that Monday until Michael came for me. My mother backed me up. I have an iron-clad alibi, but that seems to have slipped your feeble mind.''

''Your alibi has a hole in it big enough to drive an eighteen-wheeler through. Your mother napped in the afternoon. You told me that yourself. You went to the lodge and returned while she was asleep, and she never knew you were gone.''

''Get out of here! I'm going to call my lawyer and sue you for breaking into my house.''

''Don't touch that phone.'' Mitch's voice was low but so ominous that she jerked back as though the phone on the desk were on fire.

''I didn't do it, I tell you! Oh, shit...'' Her voice had tears in it suddenly. ''I just broke up with Michael, and now you're accusing me of murder!'' She pulled open a desk drawer and Mitch reached for his gun. But she only wanted a tissue. She jerked it from its box and wiped her nose. "You must have been working too hard," she said finally. "Even if I did kill Graham—which I *didn't*—that has nothing to do with your daughter being next door. You said she wasn't there until days after Graham died."

Mitch stared at her. He could hardly think with the pounding in his head, and he could feel himself shaking inside. She wasn't going to break. She wasn't going to tell him where Emily was. He had never known such impotent rage. He wanted to drag her across the desk, to squeeze the information out of her. But the saner part of his mind knew that if he touched her, he might not be able to keep himself from really hurting her. He would be the one hauled into court, and he still wouldn't have found Emily. Time was of the essence. He had to keep hammering at her with words until she weakened.

"Nila Ridge called you last Friday night and told you that she'd seen you at the lodge the afternoon Graham died. She tried to blackmail you. You agreed to a meeting here Tuesday evening, and you killed her."

The color drained slowly from her face. "You *are* crazy," she whispered. "Why are you saying these things? None of it happened."

"I don't know if you killed her here," Mitch went on relentlessly, "or in those woods the other side of the lodge where we found her body. More likely it was there. Nila was small, but so are you. You'd have had a hard time getting the body into the car alone and dragging it off the road into the woods. And you'd have been in a hurry to get Nila away from the house before your mother came home. You must have forced Nila to drive her car to the woods at gunpoint. After you killed her and tried to cover her body with leaves, you hid her car and walked back here, cutting across the lodge grounds. When you got back, you realized that Emily was staying next door, that she could have seen you and Nila leaving. Or maybe you didn't learn about that until today.''

Her gaze, which had been fixed with a kind of sick fascination on his face, suddenly darted to the door behind him. Mitch turned and saw LaDonna Thornton, in a long yellow robe, gripping the edge of the door facing with one hand, the other hand behind her. Her face was dazed by shock. How much had she heard?

Mitch turned back to Cara. "What did you do with the gun, Cara?''

She was still staring at her mother. Mitch heard a muffled sound behind him, and LaDonna Thornton said, "It's here, Chief Bushyhead.'' The hairs on the back of his neck stood up as he slowly turned. She held a twenty-two pistol in both hands. It was pointing unsteadily at his chest.

"Don't touch your gun, Chief Bushyhead, and don't move.''

"Mother!''

"Sit down and shut up for once in your life, Cara.''

Cara seemed incapable of movement. The pistol in LaDonna's hand wavered uncertainly. Mitch stepped to one side. If LaDonna took a shot at him, Cara would no longer be in the line of fire.

"Stop!'' The gun swung toward him. "I told you not to move.''

"Oh, God,'' Cara whispered. "What have you done, Mother?''

LaDonna's body heaved with repressed anguish. "He'd wasted his money and was going to sell the lodge."

"Graham wanted you to sell the lodge?" Cara murmured.

"Yes, but he couldn't sell without my signature." LaDonna drew a hand over a ravaged face that seemed to have aged twenty years, but the gun in the other hand continued to point at Mitch. She looked at Cara. "I couldn't agree, don't you see? I had no life until I started working at the lodge. I couldn't go back to that. I told him no. He beat me. *I'll kill you, you sniveling bitch. I'll beat you to a pulp. Again and again, until you agree. Think about that. I'll be back.*"

Mitch remembered the first night he'd been in that house with Doc Sullivan. LaDonna had been unable to stand up straight. She'd crept to the sofa like a frail, much older woman. She'd had the flu, she'd said. Her ribs were sore. Pneumonia, Doc had said, but LaDonna wouldn't let him examine her.

"Where's my daughter?" Mitch insisted.

LaDonna didn't seem to have heard him. "He kept hitting me and hitting me. I was on the floor. I tried to crawl away. *How about a kick in the ribs, you spineless, groveling whore? How does that feel?*"

"How long had Graham been beating you, Mother?"

"Never before that Friday night. When he left, I crawled upstairs on my hands and knees and got in bed."

"You said you had the flu."

"I couldn't tell you the truth. I didn't want anyone to know. He was my son. I made him what he was."

"You didn't!" Cara moved around the desk but stopped when LaDonna stiffened. "He was cruel. He was always that way."

"It's my fault. My blood tainted him."

"Stop talking like that! Some people are just plain mean."

"I made him angry... he couldn't help... *See what you've done? If you didn't make me so angry, I wouldn't have to beat you all the time. It's your fault. When will you ever learn?*"

"But you said it happened only once," Cara gasped.

"Years... it went on for years. I tried so hard to please him. I cleaned the house every day...cooked his favorite dishes..."

Cara darted a bewildered look at Mitch. She didn't yet understand that LaDonna was no longer talking about Graham. LaDonna held the gun at her side now, pointing down. She seemed to have forgotten she had it.

"Mrs. Thornton," Mitch said quietly, "why don't you give me the gun."

Her eyes were fixed, unfocused, on Mitch. "Oscar's... it's Oscar's gun. I'd forgotten all about it until she called."

"Nila Ridge?"

"She said she saw me leaving the lodge that afternoon."

"You told Cara not to disturb you, that you'd be napping. Then you walked to the lodge, opened the door to Graham's suite with your key, changed the insulin in the NPH bottle, and walked back."

"Cara was in her room. I used the side door. It was snowing."

"But Nila Ridge saw you."

"She wanted money. She couldn't keep up with her mortgage payments. She asked for ten thousand dollars, and that would be all, she said. But I didn't believe her. She would have been back for more, the next time she fell behind in her payments. Or she'd have told someone that she saw me leaving the lodge that afternoon."

"You told her to come here."

"I said I couldn't get the money until Tuesday. I knew Cara would be out that night. We had coffee. I put sleeping pills in her cup. When she was groggy, I walked her to her car and drove to the woods. By the time we got there, she'd passed out. I had to drag her off the road."

"And then you shot her."

She blinked as though, for an instant, she didn't recognize the room or Mitch or her daughter.

Mitch made a move toward her, and the gun jerked up. "What have you done with Emily?" he demanded fiercely.

"Emily?…sleeping pill. She saw Nila come here. She asked if Nila was a friend of mine…when she came to use the telephone. She was cold and hungry. I gave her tea and walnut cake."

"How many pills?"

"One. She's so young. She grew drowsy very quickly."

"What have you done with her? If you shot her…!"

"I couldn't. Bed…I put her to bed and tucked her in, as I used to tuck in my children. I don't know…" She shook her head slowly, and the gun dipped toward the floor again. "No end...I can't...can't kill a child...she was so sweet, so trusting."

Mitch felt the steel band that was gripping his head loosen. She was saying that she hadn't shot Emily, merely given her a sleeping pill. One pill.

"Mother, why didn't you tell me what was going on? Why didn't you tell someone?"

"No! Couldn't! *I'll punish you if you tell. You bring it on yourself. Get up and stop sniveling. Come here and let me fix it now. You want me to fix it, don't you, LaDonna? Take your clothes off and get down on your knees. You know what I like.*"

"What's she saying?" Cara whispered.

"*I'm so sore...please, don't...don't hurt me... please let me...let me rest.*"

"He can't hurt you anymore," Mitch said.

"*Be a good wife, LaDonna...do as I say...on your knees, that's right.... Oh, yes,...yes...*"

Cara's face was rigid with shock.

"Hate him. Hate Oscar. Years and years, he beat me. I was no good. Didn't know how to please my husband. I couldn't help it. I hated him. Graham was like him. It was my fault because I was too weak to leave Oscar and take the children. I hated him, but I was afraid of him. When he died...I was glad."

"No!" Cara lunged for her mother. "Liar!"

Mitch lunged, too, but not in time to wrestle the gun from LaDonna before it went off. Cara screamed and staggered back and fell against the desk, clutching her shoulder.

LaDonna dropped the gun as Cara slumped to the floor in a sitting position. Blood seeped between the fingers still clutching her shoulder. LaDonna crumpled to her knees beside her daughter. "Cara? I didn't mean . . . oh, no . . . my little girl."

"Let her lie down," Mitch said. He lowered Cara to the floor. She was conscious and moaning softly. Mitch pried her fingers from her shoulder and examined the wound. "Looks like the bullet just grazed her." He looked around at LaDonna, who still knelt on the floor, both hands covering her mouth. She started to scream.

Mitch grabbed her shoulders and shook her hard. "Get a grip on yourself! You have to call an ambulance for Cara."

Her eyes were wide, staring, but she stopped screaming. She focused on Mitch. "The ambulance," she said, "I have to call." She caught the edge of the desk and pulled herself to her feet.

"Tell me where my daughter is."

"Basement," LaDonna murmured as she lifted the receiver. "Stairs in the utility room. Key's on the hook beside the door."

Mitch picked up the twenty-two pistol. "You can't run away, Mrs. Thornton."

She looked at him disbelievingly, fully with him now. "I couldn't leave my daughter like this."

Mitch nodded and ran from the study, down the hall, and through the kitchen. The key was where she'd said it would be. He unlocked the door, fumbled for the light switch, and raced down the dim stairs. Emily was asleep on a narrow bed, covered up to her chin. She was breathing evenly. She looked peaceful.

Tears stung Mitch's eyes as he shook her gently. "Emily . . . baby . . . wake up."

She mumbled and tried to push his hands away. Mitch lifted her to a sitting position. "Wake up, sweetheart. Talk to me."

Her heavy eyelids fluttered. "Daddy?"

"Yes, I'm here. I'm going to take you upstairs. We'll go home soon."

"Home?" she said numbly. Her heavy-lidded eyes tried to focus on Mitch's face. "I wanted to go home. I was going to call you... I asked... a woman, she... Oh, Daddy!" She threw her arms around him and buried her face in his jacket, holding on to him for dear life. "I'm sorry... I'm so sorry. I love you, Daddy."

He hugged her so hard she gasped for breath. "I love you, too, sweetheart," he said brokenly.

"What happened? Where is this place?"

"Mrs. Thornton's basement. She's upstairs waiting for an ambulance for her daughter. I'll explain everything later."

She yawned and rubbed her eyes with the heel of one hand. "How did you find me?"

"Temple and Kevin came out to the Roberts place to get you. When they couldn't find you, they came to me."

She clung to him again and said sleepily, "I missed you. I've been so immature, Daddy."

"You were right to be mad at me. I should have told you I was seeing Lisa. After you found out, I should have talked to you more then, too. I let the investigation interfere. Come on, now. Can you walk, or do you want me to carry you?"

She released him reluctantly and got to her feet, swaying. "Wow, my head feels weird."

"She gave you a sleeping pill. It'll wear off pretty soon."

Emily frowned in bewilderment.

"She was desperate, sweetheart. Even so, when it came down to it, she couldn't really hurt you. Thank God!"

She shook her head. "I don't understand any of this, Daddy."

"You will later. You ready?"

She nodded. They went up the narrow stairs, Mitch's arm around her, holding her steady and close. As they topped the stairs and entered the utility room, Mitch heard the wind rattle against a window, heard its mournful howl. He closed his eyes for a second and saw Emily lying, as still as death, on the narrow cot in the dim basement. He would see her like that for a long time, like an image from a recurring nightmare.

In the distance, an ambulance siren rose above the sound of the wind.

Flight to
YESTERDAY
VELDA JOHNSTON

A NIGHTMARE REVISITED

Dubbed a "young Jean Harris" by the press, Sara Hargreaves spent four years in prison for a crime of passion she didn't commit. Now she's escaped, and she's desperate to clear her name and to see her dying mother.

As her face appears nightly on the local news, Sara disguises herself, and with the help of a young law student she is forced to trust, she returns to the scene of the crime.

The fashionable sanatorium where handsome plastic surgeon Dr. Manuelo Covarrubias was stabbed with a knife bearing Sara's fingerprints looks much the same. But as Sara begins her flight to yesterday, the secrets surrounding the callous playboy doctor who jilted her unfold. Secrets that once drove someone to murder...secrets that could kill again.

MYSTERY WRITERS OF AMERICA GRAND MASTER

HUGH PENTECOST

A PIERRE CHAMBRUN MYSTERY

MURDER IN HIGH PLACES

Larry Welch, a well-known journalist, is putting on a
story so big it could lead to international
disaster—or even war.

He seeks sanctuary in New York's luxurious Hotel
Beaumont to decide his story's fate, throwing legendary
manager Pierre Chambrun into the biggest
crisis of his career.

"A tale of mounting suspense, some glamour
and, inevitably, murder."
—*Kansas City Star*

Can you keep a secret?

You can keep this one plus 2 free novels.

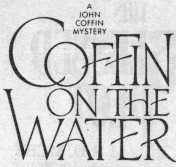

THIS BLESSED PLOT

M.R.D. MEEK
A LENNOX KEMP MYSTERY

Rich and poor. Lennox Kemp knew they all had their peculiarities. On the other side of the tracks—although disguised behind fine crystal and patrician smiles—were the Courtenays.

Twins Vivian and Venetia were rich, reckless and probably quite ruthless. They needed Kemp to oversee the legalities of the rather bizarre plans for their massive inheritance....

"M.R.D. Meek moves ever closer to the charmed company of Ruth Rendell and P. D. James."

—*Detroit News*